DEAR MASTER

by
Terry Smith

GW00995274

SILVER MINK BOOKS
An Imprint of Silver Moon

PO Box CR25 Leeds LS7 3TN
and
PO Box 1614 New York NY 10156

New authors welcome

Printed and bound in Great Britain

SILVER MINK is an imprint of SILVER MOON BOOKS
of LEEDS

*[Silver Moon Books of Leeds and Silver Moon Books of London
are in no way connected]*

**If you like one of our books you will probably like
them all!**
To order other titles see details and extracts on back
pages

**For free 20 page booklet of extracts from previous books
(and, if you wish to be on our confidential mailing list,
from forthcoming monthly titles as they are published)
please write to:-**

Silver Moon Reader Services
PO Box CR 25 LEEDS LS7 3TN
or
PO Box 1614 NEW YORK NY 10156

Surely the most erotic freebie ever!!

DEAR MASTER first published 1995
Copyright Terry Smith 1995
The right of Terry Smith to be identified as author of this work has been asserted in accordance with
sections 77 and 78 of the Copyright Designs and Patents Act 1988

DEAR MASTER
Terry Smith

For Geof Clarke -
My oldest friend and the best storyteller I know

This is fiction - in real life, practice safe sex

Every little girl knows about love. It is only her capacity to suffer because of it that increases.
    Françoise Sagan.

CHAPTER 1

The more certain Susan Dixon became that the stranger with whom she shared an otherwise empty carriage in the hurtling train was using her reflection in the night-blackened window to aid his masturbation, the more excited she became herself.

She tried to see herself through the stranger's eyes. Although she was twenty-two years old with a well rounded 34" bust, she knew that at 5' 2" she was quite small and that her petite body and youthful looks meant that she could easily pass for a school girl.

What made her want to dress like a child? For some reason, last year, when her mother and father were killed in the car crash, she had suddenly reverted, as if she wanted to be back in a time when she was their little girl and the world was safe with them to protect her from its evils and tell her what to do.

Her golden blond locks were clipped short and layered in a natural ruffled look which gave her the appearance of a street urchin who seldom bothered with the vanity of combing her hair. Her radiant skin and naturally rosy cheeks were the result of a healthy diet and regular daily exercise. They were so fresh and clear that anything but the lightest make-up would have ruined them. She seldom wore lipstick and her wide innocent baby-blue eyes could hardly have been more arresting.

Today she wore a plain white blouse and black skirt and stockings under her calf length stone coloured mac. Only her high heeled black patent leather shoes gave her age away. So the middle-aged man in the other corner was fantasising about having sex with a wide-eyed innocent of fourteen. How wicked! It made Susan shudder with excitement.

The edges of the stranger's overcoat were drawn together, hiding his suit and hands: and something else, the true form and size of which Susan could only speculate about in the wild exaggerations of her imagination. She could see the regular almost imperceptible movement beneath the thick wool of the coat, and the muscle which nervously moved in the cheek of his face when he approached too close to his ultimate goal. When that happened, he stopped and sat perfectly still, only the still twitching facial muscle providing evidence that he wasn't made of stone.

He didn't look at her directly, but his eyes never left her reflection in the window, and her eyes never left his. Although they were at least ten feet apart, she was totally under his control, just as surely as if he held her captive at the end of a lead.

'Open your coat, open your coat, open your coat,' the wheels of the carriage seemed to say.

And ever so slowly, almost as if hypnotised into doing something against her will, she opened her legs until her knees were a foot apart and then she unbuttoned her coat and pulled it aside to reveal her white blouse and black mini skirt. And the rhythm of the rails started to sing a different tune.

'Raise your skirt, raise your skirt, raise your skirt.'

Slowly, she began to inch her skirt up towards her waist. She didn't dare look down, but she could imagine how the tiny triangle of her white knickers and the pale flesh of her bare thighs must look to him, when contrasted against the

6

deep shiny black of her fifteen-denier stockings. She lifted
her bottom and rolled her skirt up to her waist. She held it
there with hands which shook, and slowly opened her legs
further, until at last the most private corner of her body was
held wide open to his gaze. Only then did she look down.
And she wasn't at all surprised or embarrassed to see that
her vagina had eaten part of her knickers, and drawn them
tight between the golden curls on either side.

She watched the frantic movement beneath his coat,
matched by the twitching muscle in his face. The sensation
of heat and movement humming throughout her own body
was almost unbearable now. She knew that she shouldn't
go any further. She knew that she shouldn't have come this
far. But she was helpless to resist. More than anything else
in the world she wanted to remove her knickers and present
her swollen naked vulva to his gaze.

Her fingers moved from her skirt and across the burning flesh of her belly to her left thigh. She unbuttoned the
suspender straps one at a time; watching how his eyes half
closed as each one came free, as if their removal caused
him physical pain deep down inside his crotch.

They followed the same ritual on her right thigh, and
now only her knickers remained. She placed both thumbs
under the thin waist band of her briefs and waited, ensur-
ing that he was ready. Then, she pressed down with her
heels and shoulders to lift her bottom free of the seat and,
with one swift movement, she peeled them away from her
clinging vagina. He almost looked as if he was mortally
wounded now. His face was pale, yet covered in sweat, and
his mouth was open in a silent cry of pain. But his eyes
willed her on and spoke to her of his urgent need. How
much longer could he delay? He mustn't ruin it; not when
they had come this far together.

She pushed the knickers to her knees, then sent them
sailing over the abyss and felt them slide effortlessly down

the sheer nylon slopes of her legs and lodge at her ankles. They didn't make a sound. There wasn't a sound anywhere now, as the world waited for her to open her legs. She stepped out of the knickers with her left leg, feeling them slip from her ankle. And now she was free. Free to do what he wanted her to do. Free to do what she wanted to do; free for the first time in her life.

Slowly she turned a little more towards him and began on the slow journey to move her legs apart. She could feel the cloying stickiness of her own juices and hear the squelching sound inside her vagina as the thickly coated walls were pulled away from each other. Her legs moved inexorably apart with all the slow ordained dignity of a pair of mechanical lock gates opening to receive an ocean liner.

She had never ever felt this wicked. She knew what must happen next. She hadn't known when the stranger's dark magnetism and the rhythm of the rails had forced her to disrobe. But it seemed so obvious now. As her legs reached their ultimate width apart and she made quite certain, with one last effort, that she couldn't open herself up any further to his hungry gaze; she knew then what she must do next.

He would lead and she would follow. And they would masturbate together and reach simultaneous climaxes. They would come at the same time and enjoy the excitement of a shared orgasmic experience without ever having touched, or spoken, or known each other in any way at all, except in their parallel fantasies.

And then - the stranger was on his feet! Panic! Confusion! Susan automatically closed her coat as she realised that someone was coming, had come, was in the coach with them.

The stranger was scrambling to retrieve his briefcase, hat, and cane. And the next moment he was gone. And now the confusion in Susan's mind was heightened by the sound of squealing brakes and protesting metal as the train wheels quickly slowed for the approaching station.

She felt the shock of a clumsy hand giving her shoulder a glancing blow, as someone lurched past her, using the back of her seat to steady themselves against the decelerating motion of the train. The guard! It was the guard staring aggressively after the stranger, who was hurrying away down the platform without a backwards glance.

Susan was wild eyed and flushed and acutely aware of her aroused state and near total nakedness beneath her coat. And when the guard looked down at her, she could see from his expression that he would have liked to question her.

His eyes moved from hers and travelled slowly down her body. It was as if they could see right through her coat and she clenched her jaw as she struggled to stop her right leg from shaking. She moved her leg back so that the ankle bearing her knickers would be out of sight beneath the seat, all the time hardly daring to breath or hope that he wouldn't notice. And all the time her useless brain could only think of her hot swollen vulva, all glistening and damp in its nakedness.

She was sure that the steaming heat of her arousal must be percolating up between the gap where the edges of her unbuttoned coat met, bringing the pungent intimate scent of her to his distended nostrils. She was sure that it must be that all pervading aroma which was holding him transfixed, staring at her lap.

What would he do if she opened her coat and revealed herself to him; naked, hot, and available? Would he be able to resist taking advantage of her?

Or would he chastise her as she deserved, chastise a filthy wanton whore, take her across his knee perhaps and ...

His lips moved and she heard the words, but she didn't understand what they meant until he repeated them again.

"Ticket please, Miss."

Was he wondering how old she was? Probably. She must look like a dishevelled child.

"Six minutes to your stop, Miss."

"Thank you."

She didn't look round, but she listened to him move away, going back along the train in the direction he had come. Only then did she glance over her shoulder to make sure he had really left the carriage.

He had done nothing about her wickedness.

But the wheels were talking again.

A naughty girl must be punished ...

Punished ...

Punished ...

Punished ...

Then, as they slowed to a stop she saw the book that the stranger, in his embarrassment, had left.

CHAPTER 2

It took Susan three days to finish the book and it had a dramatic affect on her life. In those early days, she was sure that she would soon see her stranger again. Her heart lifted in hope at each station as her darting eyes searched for him amongst the crowd of passengers waiting on the platform, but he was never there.

At first she consoled herself with the knowledge that she would soon be curled up on the sofa with his book, but that soon palled. She knew the story by heart now and needed something more. It taught her a lot though. She had realised that her sexual fantasies had always involved being in a state of helplessness in the clutches of a dominant male who beat her and forced her to make love to him against her will. But she had always accepted that they were just fantasies and would remain as such. Now she knew that there were other people out there who had similar fantasies to her own, and similar sexual needs. And more importantly: that sometimes, somehow, they found each other.

With her parents recently dead, she was totally alone. Only her own thoughts for company. But her thoughts now included those of the author. And it wasn't only his erotic descriptions which had excited her, it was what he was telling her to do. She knew he was right; cowards have a miserable wasted life: be brave enough to take life by the throat and live it to the full.

She made a pact with herself: at least once a week she would go naked under her coat, and at least once a week she would masturbate in a public place where there was a possibility of discovery!

Time passed, and now the winter seemed colder and bleaker than ever. She rose in the dark and returned home in the dark. Coming back to an empty house which was completely indifferent to the loneliness inside her, she felt like a shipwrecked sailor dying of thirst. All round her there were good looking men who showed their interest, but none of them could quench her special kind of thirst for the sort of fulfilment the dark stranger could have given her.

But it was a different kind of thirst which made her brave the crowds in the little shop by the station. She had started to drink more. She intended to do something about it, but just at the moment she seemed to need the comfort of the extra intake. So, she went into the shop to buy a couple of cans of larger for the journey home. But she also went in there as part of the pact which she had made with herself; to try to turn herself from a mouse in to a tiger. Almost every day now, she went to the loo before leaving work and took off everything except her suspender belt, stockings, and high heeled shoes, before donning a thick outdoor coat.

She had only been in this shop once before and hadn't enjoyed the experience. At this time in the evening, it was full of a constantly changing writhing mass of noisy commuters, all intent on buying their drinks, cigarettes, and newspapers, for the train journey home to Essex. She had hated all the shoving and shouting. And she had especially disliked running the gauntlet of the young city yobs who insisted on reducing the already meagre space yet further. They crowded round the boxes of canned beer stacked in the middle of the floor, crowing like roosters about their prowess with women, booze, and cars.

With her mind acutely aware of her nakedness and vulnerability beneath her coat, it should prove to be a worthy test of her resolve to become a tiger. It might even be possible to loose herself in a corner, as if searching the shelves for something she couldn't find, and slip a hand inside the join of her buttoned coat.

So, she nipped into the untidy little shop and reached a hand into the rugby scrum of sweating masculinity around the piles of canned beer. And it was then, when she raised her eyes as she emerged clutching two cans of Carlesberg Special Brew, that something registered on her subconscious mind. She didn't know what it was at first, only that she had seen something familiar which had lit up a light inside her head. It was the familiar livery which she recognised. Up there on the top shelf, next to the magazines full of naked women, there were a group of books with the symbol of the chain running down their spines. They were exactly like the one which the stranger had left on the train and which now resided in the drawer of her bedside table.

Her head was swimming as she made her way over to them and a moment later she was standing at the counter handing over her selections. The Asian shopkeeper's normally bored eyes flickered across her face for a moment as he turned the book over to check its price. Not for the first time she regretted how young she looked, as he decided whether to serve her to the book and the alcohol. Then, with an almost perceptible mental shrug, he rang up the sale.

She wanted him to release it to her immediately, so that she could be ready to slip it inside her copy of the Standard, but he held on to it while he rang up the other two items. And when he had finished, he told her the price of her purchases, and took a brightly coloured paper bag from under the counter and popped the book inside. She realised that she was shaking, and that he had noticed as he had taken the ten-pound note from her. For a moment she had a sudden hope that her choice of literature might have registered with him and given him some interest. But his eyes didn't even look at her as he handed her the change; his thoughts and attention were already on the next customer.

The next few weeks were very confusing for her. She plucked up the courage to buy a succession of books from the little shop, until her presence there became almost common place. They served to reinforce her growing conviction about her own sexuality. She found the thought of being bound and beaten, and forced to unquestioningly obey another's will, tremendously exciting. She longed to be part of that world. But how? None of the men she met at work, or saw on her journey, seemed remotely like that. She started to take more and more risks with her public masturbating, possibly subconsciously hoping to be caught by someone in authority who would take advantage of her. But to no avail, and probably just as well.

She returned again to the original book. The thought of belonging to the man who had written that book made her shiver with fear and longing. She didn't understand why it was, but she detected a sense of deviousness about him. She also didn't understand why that should excite her so much. But it did. Perhaps she was like those women who visited murderers in prison, or who enjoyed having sex with gangsters wearing guns strapped to their chests. She just sensed that the author knew her better than she knew herself. That he understood her need to be wicked. That if he had control of her, she wouldn't be able to hide anything from him. He would know what she really wanted and she wouldn't be able to resist him when he forced her to live out her desires.

She lay in bed looking at the cover on the book. She was tired of masturbating, and soon it would be too warm for a top coat. This little book had seemed to hold out such promise for her future when she had first found it. But it had all come to nothing. Suddenly, she sat bolt upright. What if she wrote to the publishers and asked them to pass a letter on to the author? Would they do it? And what was more to the point, would he reply?

He likes shaven women, she thought.

The next day she bought depilation cream. And that night she sat on the bed and surrounded herself with Can-Can, her toy panda, and all his little Gonk friends. Then they all watched intently as she propped her mother-of-pearl backed hand mirror up in front of her and removed her beautiful golden curls. She started by using her fingers to make herself very wet, and then, when her vulva was swollen and firm, she used the nail scissors followed by the razor. She took her time and kept stopping to rub her clitoris and watch herself in the mirror. Once her vulva was bald, she stopped and pored herself a drink so that she could walk about the house and examine herself in the many mirrors. She walked towards them, trying not to appear self conscious, but carefully watching the way her bald mound moved with each step she took. Then she posed for herself, turning this way and that, sometimes bending down and peering at herself from behind, sometimes with her legs open, or with one up on a dining chair.

She returned to the bedroom and stood in front of the dressing table mirror and asked the advice of her fury bedtime friends. She ran her fingers over her bald pubic mound and all round her vulva. It felt strange. The razor had cut close, but she could still feel the tops of little bristly hairs every here and there. She closed her legs tightly together. If she moved the mirror down so that she could only see herself from the waist, was it possible to imagine she was a pre-pubescent child?

She moved the mirror back up again and opened her legs wide and once more stared at her bald vulva. It seemed strangely unfinished, but once she used the creams she would

15

be as naked as a coot there for several months. Her vulva would be as soft and smooth as a baby's bottom.

She sat on the edge of the bed and watched herself in the mirror as she applied the creams. Then she took just as much care over the rest of her appearance, and looked at herself several times before buttoning her coat for the last time. Her preparations had taken a long time, but she was finally ready to walk back to the station and use the photo booth. She was now so used to going without any clothes beneath her coat that it took very little extra courage to pose like that for the automatic camera. This had long been another of her fantasies. She had always wanted some photos of herself taken while she was still young and looking at her best.

She even took some of herself masturbating. It wasn't hard. She only had to imagine the curtain suddenly being torn back to reveal a man standing there. The angry guard, or the vagrant with the dreadlocks who always shouted after her, they were her favourite fantasies. But, despite her secret desires, she was always careful afterwards to stand close guard over the delivery chute while she waited for the pictures to be developed. Although her mother was dead, her training wasn't. She could clearly hear the strident nagging voice in her head just as if she was still there: 'You can never be too careful Susan. You don't want strangers looking over your shoulder at your private snaps, and you never know when there might be a sudden breeze.'

The next night she wrote the two letters. Then she chose the photos and added them, and a lock of her shorn hair, to the author's letter and placed it in a sealed envelope. She placed that inside the envelope addressed to the publisher, along with her letter of explanation, and everything was done. It only remained now to pop it in the post.

She took to taking a turn around the block before bed time. She was taking a chance, a loan woman walking at night, especially if any would-be rapists had known what lay beneath her coat. But it excited her to carry the letter in her pocket, and hold it up to each of the two post boxes she passed, pretending that one day she would have the courage to release it.

And then one night it was gone! She heard it drop on top of the others inside the box. She didn't know if it was an accident, or if she had always intended to do it one day. But anyway, it was done. And tomorrow it would be on its way, and Her Majesty's mail would have the honour of asking the unknown author if he would allow her to be his slave.

Susan placed the envelope on her dressing table, propping it against the ample stomach of Boggle, her favourite Gonk.

Boggle's crossed-eyes peered at her from behind small round wire spectacles balanced on a huge bulbous nose set in a bright purple face surrounded by a halo of luminous green hair spikes. As usual, he looked lost and bemused by the world around him. It was a feeling which she had always shared, but which seemed to have increased since the death of her parents.

She had longed for this moment: and dreaded it. At first she had thought about it constantly, but later, she had convinced herself it would never come. Now it had, and she felt terrified. Not just nervous, or scared. But actually terrified of what the envelope might contain. She had no doubt it was from him. She had no one else to write to her. She had studied the post mark, it had been posted the day before in Kent. Is that where she would be living soon? It seemed like tempting fate to even hope.

She undressed in the bathroom and showered, all the time, trying to remain calm. Once she had dried herself, she ran her hand between her legs to be sure she remained perfectly smooth and hairless. Then she brushed her hair and applied fresh make-up. She had taken as much trouble over her appearance as she would have done if it had been the man himself waiting for her in the bedroom, not just a letter from him. And why not? She had nothing else to take trouble over, but his letter could alter all that. It might dash all her hopes, but then again, it could invite her into a new life which, until now, she could only fantasise about. She wrapped herself in the towel and walked quickly to the bedroom.

The envelope was still there, with Boggle gazing shortsightedly over the top of it, and she started to shake again. She let the towel drop to the floor and looked at herself in the mirror, trying to imagine what he would think of her. She looked so pale, she thought. Such white skin, with a light crazing of blue veins round her inner thighs. It made them look so cool, as if they were made of marble.

And between them, the smooth bald hill, without even the glint of a hair on it. It looked so small. Even her own cupped hand could hide it from sight. Her eyes moved down it searching for the split between her lips, but there was no evidence of it. She looked as unfinished as a Barbie doll. Her eyes lifted up to the twin domes of her breasts, with the swollen nipples giving her body its first touch of colour. Such a light pink, softer than a flamingo's feathers. They would darken to brown, if she ever had a baby. But for now they would remain light pink, as testimony that she was still little more than a virgin child.

Her gaze continued up, and on to her face. Here at last there was some warmth. And also some colour, from the small touch of make-up and the startling shining halo of golden hair. 'Like spun gold,' her father had always said. Not that he had known it like this. She had always worn her hair long, before his untimely death. That wasn't quite true. The truth was that they had never allowed her to have it cut. Perhaps they'd been right. It had used to spill down over her shoulders and breasts, like a shimmering golden waterfall. Perhaps she would grow it again. She remembered back to a time when she had been a little girl; her hair had been shoulder length then, and her father had brushed it for her every night. He had enjoyed pulling the brush through its thick waves, over and over again, in a soothing monotony which made her ready to crawl into bed and listen dozily to his soft rounded voice reading her a bed-time story.

Yes, she was pretty. Almost too pretty. She was almost exactly like a full sized Barbie doll now, with her near perfect looks and apparent lack of vagina. Except that she looked younger. Barbie was a young woman, whereas she looked barely old enough to have reached her teens.

Her body had never looked better. It was as near perfect as God, diet, and daily exercise could make it. So if he didn't want it, there was nothing she could do about it. She had done her best.

She picked the envelope up with shaking hands and looked over her shoulder, checking her bottom in the mirror as she walked towards the top of the bed. Did all women worry like this, always concerned about all those little things which they thought could look better? The small of her back curved right in making her tight little bottom as prominent as a molehill on a bowling green.

She sat crossed-legged on the bed holding the envelope in both shaking hands. She plucked up her courage, closed her eyes, took a deep breath, and ripped it open. There was just a single piece of folded paper, no photographs and no lock of pubic hair. She took it out and opened it up. It was no love note. It was a brief business letter which contained the few typed words which would decide her fate.

CHAPTER 3

The foyer of the motel was modern, with a stone flagged floor and a lot of natural wood and brick.

Susan looked over at the two smartly dressed young women behind the reception desk. They were preoccupied with their own conversation and she decided to pass by the fountain on the side furthest from them. She was still not used to the four inch stiletto heels. It gave her another good excuse for looking down at her feet, as if she was concentrating on avoiding the mortar joints between the paving slabs, rather than trying to avoid meeting their eyes. There were three steps down to the carpeted lounge, and standing at the top of them surveying the hand-full of early evening customers, she knew him at once.

Her mind was full of doubt as she wobbled towards him on unsteady legs and it wasn't the unfamiliarly high heels which were to blame this time. Her legs were turning to jelly again and she tried to blank out all other thoughts in an effort to complete the journey without incident. She had no idea what to say and no certainty that she still had the power of speech.

Now she was almost there, and he was rising and smiling a greeting. It had all the warmth of the watery sunlight of a frosty spring morning. He indicated a chair and she sank into it gratefully, without either of them saying a word.

He sat and looked at her and she bowed her head and returned his stare from beneath her eyelashes. The smile was still on his lips, and in the creases at the corners of his mouth, but it hadn't reached the deep brown pools which were his eyes.

When she had first seen him, from the top of the steps, she had guessed he was in his late thirties. But now she was closer, she could see he was much older: perhaps forty-five. His hair must once have been jet black, but it had long since faded and become streaked with grey and silver, making him look very distinguished.

His skin was tanned to parchment in a natural way, as if he spent long periods outside, and he had a slim body and the posture of a much younger man. He wasn't tall, or overly muscular, but he looked fit, as if he exercised regularly. And he emanated an inner peace and natural authority which would make most sensible people wary of crossing him.

She would like to have seen more, but she couldn't hold his gaze any longer and she dropped her eyes and studied the grain in the light ash table top. This wasn't the stranger from the train, which she had half hoped it might be. But she was glad of that, now. Now she understood why his story had affected her so much. There was an aura of latent menace about him, which made her tingle all over. It was incredible, a sensation she had never experienced before, which seemed to light up her whole body and set it on edge. It was as if she had disturbed a coiled cobra and was now waiting for it to strike. She could hear the blood roaring like a waterfall in her ears and feel the heat rising in her body. And if he didn't stop looking at her, and say something soon, she really felt as if she might swell up until she exploded.

She sensed him move and glanced up quickly. He had finished his initial appraisal of her and was smiling more kindly now, in a condescending way. Deep creases had appeared at the corner of each eye, like footprints left by a small bird blessed with an over abundance of toes. He nodded a silent command at her and she felt her heart jump and settle in her mouth, almost choking her. Her eyes darted to either side, as if looking for escape. She had no intention of refusing him. It was only the unexpectedness of it which made her hesitate. That, and the fact that it had been a long journey for a person in her state of arousal, and she had expected to have been allowed time to freshen up.

Her hands shook so much that as her fingers fumbled to undo her coat she was grateful that its buttons were no smaller. She took one last glance round, but she had already confirmed that he had chosen their seats well and the high back of her chair ensured that there was no possibility of them being overlooked. Then she opened her coat and revealed herself to him. His expression didn't change, but she knew he was pleased with her, and she took a moment to glory in the wonderful sensations which were filling her mind and body. It was too gorgeously wicked to think about now. She would go over it second by second when she was safely on her own. It was enough, for now, to recognise that he was the most sensational man she could possibly have hoped to meet. And that these first moments with him had been more exciting than her wildest fantasy. It couldn't possibly last. Nothing this good ever did. But she knew that it was going to get better for a long time yet, before it began to pall.

"Would you like to come for me?" Susan bit her lip on hearing the softly spoken words and nodded as she realised that that was precisely what she did want to do.

She was already extremely wet. And she had no doubt, that the thought of her situation sitting here naked under the control of this magnificent man, would soon allow her to drive herself over the top. She let go of her coat, and gripping the edge of the table with her left hand, she started to masturbate. She let her love for him well up from deep inside until every part of her body was shuddering with ecstasy and screaming out to give itself to him. She started to whimper between her tightly closed lips and she vaguely hoped it wasn't really as loud as it sounded to her as it echoed round inside her head.

Her eyes glazed over and started to role. She was no longer sure of her surroundings as she left the motel lounge behind and entered her own world where anything was possible. All she could see now were the two points of bright light deep within the limpid brown pools of his eyes as they grew together and started to bore deep into her brain. Now she was well beyond the point when she could have exercised any restraint and she pushed herself on towards those twin points of light deep inside the blackness of his eyes.

And at last, when she came, she was diving down into those deep, dark, secret pools and falling head over heels into the fluffy marshmallow clouds where she would be safe for ever.

Her mouth was forced open in a huge silent gasp and her back arched as her hips jerked uncontrollably. She expected his eyes to leave her for a moment and survey the room, to see if anyone had noticed her enforced tribal dance. But they didn't. In fact, they barely blinked as he continued to watch her jerking body with quiet dispassion. His uncommitted expression drove her on harder and further, forcing her to try to make him understand what was happening to her and how much she wanted to please him and receive his approval. She was totally wanton and abandoned now and still his cold indifference drove her on and on. Until at last, she achieved total satisfaction and was full to overflowing with both shame and joy in proportions which ensured her perfect bliss.

"Good girl. Did you enjoy that?"

Susan barely dared to look at him. She was breathless and flushed and much too ashamed to speak. She could hardly believe it was real. She had just climaxed on command, in front of a complete stranger. And now he had asked her a question in a matter-of-fact tone, just like a bored new acquaintance at a dinner party breaking the ice by discussing the weather. Her natural instinct was to hide her true emotions, but it was no good lying to this man. She didn't want to make him angry. He wouldn't let her off. He knew her better than she knew herself and he was going to use that knowledge and power to hurt her. She knew that. That was partly why she was here. That, and the chance for love.

She looked at him. He was calm and composed, dressed in impeccable casual clothes, breathing in the scent of his brandy before taking a sip as he waited for her reply. But she also saw herself: flushed in face and breast, with the wild look of desperation still in her eyes and the pungent aroma from her wet thighs making her nostrils curl. She needed him. Her whole body hummed with an excitement which she had never experienced before. Was it love? She didn't know. But she did know this was her one chance for a life which meant anything, and whatever happened, she mustn't loose it. She would be as submissive as he required. Perhaps even as submissive as she desired.

She nodded to show that she had. There, she had admitted it, and it was bliss. He didn't condemn her for her unusual desires. He understood her completely. He understood her need to be abused, mistreated, and dominated, and he was willing to indulge her. Her head sang with the possibilities of their future together. What humiliations would he make her endure? When she looked into his eyes, she knew they would be much worse than anything she could possibly think of for herself. Perhaps even worse than anything she could stand. She did hope so.

Satisfied, he took something from the inside pocket of his jacket and placed it on the table before her.

"Button your coat," he instructed, and waited until she had done so before continuing. "This is a contract which I

24

want you to read while I order you a drink. What would you like?"

"A gin and tonic, please." Susan was pleased she had found the courage to speak to him at last.

"Call me master," he instructed her.

Susan felt her heart jump again. It wasn't just a game with him. He really meant it. She had assumed they would discuss role playing, and what humiliation and pain she was prepared to permit. Perhaps that was still the case, but something told her it wasn't. Something told her that if she submitted now she would really be his slave, not just a week-end indulgence.

"I'm sorry, Master." Her voice almost croaked with emotion.

His nod was almost imperceptible, but it made her glow with pleasure. She so wanted to please him. She wanted to show him she could be the best slave in the world.

He raised his arm to call for the waitress, who responded at once. When she arrived, he indicated with a nod that it was Susan who wanted to order. The girl was dressed in a white shirt, with bow tie, very tight black trousers and a brightly coloured waistcoat, and when she turned her back to him, Susan noticed that he let his eyes languidly examine her pert little bottom.

"Gin and tonic, please." Susan's voice betrayed the fact that she had taken an instant dislike to this rival for his attention.

"With ice and a slice?"

"Yes please."

"Thank you."

It only took a moment, but it was long enough to let Susan know she would be insanely jealous of every other woman he looked at.

"And nothing for you, Sir?" the girl turned to him again.

He smiled, as if her persistent persuasive charm had induced him to change his mind in order to please her.

"Another brandy."

"Thank you, Sir," and she turned, so that Susan would see the triumphant sparkle in her eyes as she went to fetch their drinks.

"Do you want to read it?"

"Could you tell me what it says, please, Master?"

He shrugged his shoulders. "More or less that you belong to me and that I, or anyone I stipulate, can do anything they damn well please to you, short of actually killing you. If you sign it, you are signing your entire freedom away. You will belong to me body and soul and I can sell or give your contract to anyone else I choose."

"Is it legal, Master?"

"Probably not, but my friends and I shall treat it as if it were. And it certainly is enforceable, which is more important. I advise you most strongly not to sign it unless you genuinely intend to honour it."

"What will happen if I don't sign it, Master?"

"Nothing. There's no coercion. If you want to hang on to your freedom and take your chance that life will come good, don't sign it. If you want to take your chance with me and whoever comes after me, then sign it. But either way, it must be because that's what you want."

"I would like to sign it please, Master."

"Be certain. This is a contract with the Devil, for ever. There can be no divorce."

Susan nodded. "I know. I want to be yours completely, for ever, please, Master."

The waitress returned dead on cue with their drinks and a few minutes later both copies of the contract were signed and witnessed and Susan belonged completely to her master, for ever: heart, mind, body, and soul. But especially, heart.

Susan stood in her master's study in awe of her surroundings. The night had been too dark for her to make out much of the countryside they had passed through on their journey, but as they had started to ascend the slight hill, she had seen the dark outline of the windmill against the orange glow of the sky and thrilled at the thought that he might live there. Now she was inside it and it was all she could have hoped for. The room they were in was about twenty five feet by fifteen and constructed almost entirely from wood, with oak pillars, beams and rafters, but it was cut short on one side in a very unusual way, by a wall of thick dark glass which acted like a black mirror.

One end of the room was dominated by a large leather topped partners desk, surrounded by bookcases crammed full of books. Opposite it, at the other end of the room, stood a cluster of arm chairs and two sofas, all upholstered in wine red leather. The polished plank floor was covered in Persian rugs, and three sparkling crystal chandeliers hung down on long chains from the apex of the roof. It was a strange mixture, with the opulence of the furnishings contrasting strikingly with the, rude, unfinished, fabric of the building, but it worked, superbly. All except for the glass wall, which, once the full length tapestry curtains had been drawn back from it by some unseen motor, looked even more out of place than ever, and left a question in her mind.

She looked at it now, seeing the dull reflection of the brightly lit room and the figure of herself and her master in its impenetrable darkness, and wondered at its purpose. But as she watched, the reflection of her master moved. It crossed to the desk, and the next moment the room behind the glass was bathed in light. At least fifteen feet below the level of the study, the cold discomfort of the stone floor of the other room wasn't reduced by any soft warm rugs, and nor were there any opulent furnishings to relieve the stark harshness

27

of the roughly finished stone and wood of the walls and partitions. Even without all the paraphernalia of the torturer's art, which stood on the bare floor or hung from the walls and cross-beams, there was no mistaking this hidden room for what it was: a dungeon for a very special kind of prisoner.

Susan's eyes were drawn to the one patch of colour in the whole room, where a brass bedstead with a patchwork quilt sat on a small oblong of carpet. On one side of the bed there was a table with a lamp, and on the other, what looked like a brightly painted toy cupboard. A large friendly looking teddy bear had pride of place at the head of the bed, and a pair of white baby-doll pyjamas with lace trimmed knickers were laid out further down, all ready and waiting to greet their owner when she arrived all warm and pink from her bath.

Susan turned from the relative comfort of that part of the room, to look at the huge wooden wheel which dominated the other part of the dungeon. It was the human equivalent of the gerbil's exercise wheel, but constructed from dark heavy looking timbers and iron fittings like some huge medieval siege machine. How it worked and what it was for she didn't know, but the mere sight of it filled her with a dread which made her wet between the legs in anticipation of the torturous pleasures to come.

She lay in the little bed, dressed in the baby-doll pyjamas, and pictured her master looking down on her as he stood at the glass wall of his unlit study. He had dimmed the dungeon lights, as soon as she had finished saying her prayers and climbed into bed. But the table lamp still shone out bathing her in a circle of comforting soft yellow light. The room was massive and full of unknown noises and she prayed he would be merciful and not insist that she must turn out the lamp before she fell asleep. She hugged the

28

teddy closer to her chest, feeling grateful for his presence. It had been a long time since she had knelt by the bed to say her prayers and she wasn't sure what had made her do it. Perhaps she was pandering to the gallery? There was probably something of that about her action. But it wasn't entirely for his benefit. Somehow, it had felt right to speak to God, and she had felt so much better afterwards that she knew it would become part of her nightly ritual from now on.

It was strange doing everything under his gaze. There were no ceilings anywhere, and when she had gone to the bathroom to prepare for bed, she had been grateful that the toilet was positioned next to a wall which would screen her from his view. The bath was an entirely different matter. That was positioned to give him an uninterrupted view of her, and she had taken full advantage of it, lying back and masturbating beneath the warm water certain that he would be watching her.

She should have felt ashamed of herself, but she hadn't. She belonged to him now, and that had taken away all her guilt. He was like God, sitting up there in his study, and occasionally looking down on her. And like God, he could either be pleased by her actions, or punish her if she did wrong. She wanted to please him. It gave her such a good feeling inside when she did, that it seemed like the most important thing in the world.

She had pleased him in the motel, when he had asked her how much time she needed to put her affairs in order. When she had told him she had already done so, she had seen his one eyebrow lift and felt the warmth in his voice when he had told her she was a good girl. And he had laughed for the first time when she told him she had come to him with only the clothes she stood up in; appreciating that in her case, that was very little indeed. It was a gorgeous sight and sound, which made her feel as if someone had suddenly turned the sun back on. And he had assured her she wouldn't need anything else. She smiled to herself. Yes, it was lovely to please him, but she hoped he would find time and reason to punish her sometimes, or else, she would just have to be very naughty until he did.

She hugged the teddy closer to her chest and decided she would definitely call him Oscar. His mouth had been sewn on crooked, so that on the one side he seemed to be smiling, and on the other he seemed a little stern. It could merely have been that he was made on a Friday afternoon by a seamstress who was eager to be out of the factory preparing for the start of the weekend. But Susan had a theory that there was more in life than mere humans knew about, and that teddy bears were given the expression they deserved. So her teddy needed a name which would allow him to be both kind and cross, and Oscar seemed just about perfect to her. She would treat him with true deference and respect, as befitted his stern adult status, but they would also be friends, and he would look after her at night when she was lying frightened in her bed feeling her heart beating fast. She kissed him on the nose and then put her thumb in her mouth and settled down for sleep.

CHAPTER 4

Susan awoke with the dawn the following morning; disturbed by the unfamiliar sound of the birds squabbling outside her window. Her eyes shot open and her thumb was pulled from her mouth with a plop as she struggled to remember where she was. But it was alright. She was in her own little bed in her master's house. Her wide blue eyes looked round her. In her own little bed, in her own special dungeon, at the start of a brand new day when anything might happen. She placed her thumb firmly back in her mouth and clutched at Oscar.

"What shall we do, Oscar?"

The bear swivelled his head and looked at the alarm clock. Fred Flintsone's stone club was pointing to twenty-past four.

'It's too early to disturb the master.' the gruff little voice in her head confirmed. 'We could either play, or explore.'

Both heads turned to look at the dark part of the dungeon. It was full of apparatus made of thick timbers, iron, and leather, all fixed together with steel bolts. Susan shuddered.

'Let's play!' they both decided together.

She slipped out of bed and opened the double doors of the brightly painted toy cupboard. As she had suspected, the pink shelves inside were home for a mass of dolls and cuddly toys. She looked over her shoulder, peering into the gloom of the other part of the dungeon, wondering what had disturbed her. Had she heard a sound or seen a movement? She continued to look for several seconds, but there was nothing. She was just being silly. She shivered and tried to dismiss the thought from her mind.

"Come on, there are lots of little friends for you to meet," she told Oscar, pulling him from the bed and feeling better immediately for his presence in her arms.

She would have felt safer sitting down side by side with Oscar, facing into the room, so that they could both keep an eye on the dark side of the dungeon. But that would have been silly. There was nothing nasty lurking in there, and it would only spoil her pleasure to have to look at it all the time. So Oscar sat in front of the open toy cupboard, and she knelt facing him with her back to the room.

She soon forgot her secret fears as they lost themselves in their game. As she came to know Oscar better he began to relax and become more certain of his voice and his role in her life. At first his voice had varied, not sure whether to be young and squeaky, or gruff and very grown up. But now it had assumed a middle course. It was still gruff, because that's what bears' voices are like, but deep and manly, and full of authority, as befitted one who was much older and wiser than she was. It was also mellow, kind, and caring, and full of fun. She felt much safer knowing that she had a special friend to share her fears and hopes with. And when she knew him even better, she would ask him about her master, and he would help her win his heart.

It was years since she had played with dolls and most of these were much more sophisticated than those she had owned. She had no idea that they had become so realistic these days. And she wasn't entirely sure that she approved or thought that it was necessary for them to be so correct in every detail. But, unlike herself, they all had a comprehensive wardrobe of incredibly stylish clothes and she couldn't resist examining them. Soon the dolls were all wearing a change of outfit and had sprawled out of the cupboard to take up their places sitting at ladder back chairs round their

32

own little table, ready to take elevenses with herself and Oscar.

It was at that moment that she knew she was being watched. She swung round, in fear. A big snowy haired man was looming over her. For a moment she didn't understand who he was or how he had got there. He was a heavily built man, but he had crept up almost unheard. He was smiling, but what did it mean? And what was he doing in her bedroom? Then she remembered where she was and realised that she was virtually naked in the presence of a complete stranger. She quickly covered her breasts with her hands and struggled to scramble to her feet.

He shook his head at her and she sat back down again. Whatever was going to happen, she had no doubt that he was in charge and was going to call the shots.

He continued to stare at her. And although he said nothing, she knew what he wanted. She looked round, hoping to see her master, but the stranger had come alone. Slowly she removed her hands from over her breasts and let them drop to her sides. Again, he said nothing, and gave no physical indication of his feelings, but she sensed that it was what he had wanted. His smile remained in his eyes and on his lips and she realised that he wore it as a mask; like net curtains over windows, to hide what was within.

Her breasts were now exposed through the almost transparent material of her nightdress, but his eyes didn't move to look at them. Not that that helped. In fact, it made her feel even more naked and vulnerable. He wanted her to be relaxed and behave naturally with him, she sensed that. But she couldn't. She became more embarrassed with every second. And her face and breasts started to blush and her nipples popped erect to prominently advertise her aroused state.

At last he spoke, with a faint Irish accent. And it was as if the last few minutes hadn't happened. "Hello, little girl, what a wonderful collection of dollies, are they all yours?"

His eyes ignored her condition and his words ignored what had already passed between them. He was starting from scratch as if they had just come across each other for the very first time.

Susan looked at him blankly for a moment as she slowly realised that he wanted her to play a role. He didn't seem to mind her denseness. He continued to beam down at her like an indulgent uncle with all the patience in the world to spare for a favourite niece.

"Yes. At least I think so." Susan felt very stupid, but she didn't know what else to say.

"You think so. Don't you know?"

"No, not really. I've only just arrived you see."

"Well they are. Are you pleased?"

"Oh, yes. I suppose so."

"You suppose so. You're a funny little thing aren't you? I thought you might be shy. But no one told me you were going to be quite this pretty. I'm Uncle Peter. That's what you must call me. And are you going to tell me your name?"

"Susan."

"Susan. That's a lovely name. But it's a bit grown-up for a little girl, isn't it? I think I shall call you Susie. Would you like that?"

Susan nodded her reluctant agreement. Hoping her master would soon arrive and save her from this horrible old maniac. But that wasn't sufficient for Uncle Peter.

"Yes please, Uncle Peter," he prompted her.

"Yes please, Uncle Peter," she repeated, reluctantly.

"That's better. Well, when I was told your master was preparing this lovely nursery for a very special little girl, I decided she must have some little friends to play with. So, you see, they do all belong to you." He paused, waiting for her to say something.

"Thank you, Uncle Peter," she said, wondering when this nightmare would end.

"Good. Now fetch me that one there." He pointed with his walking cane.

Susan did as she was instructed, taking care to expose as little of her naked flesh as possible to his loathsome gaze. When she returned with it and offered it to him, she realised for the first time just how big he was. He was much more than a foot taller than she was, and must have weighed more than twice as much. She estimated that he must be about fifty, but he had a ramrod straight back and a look of authority about the eyes which made her suspect that he had once been a guards' officer.

He was wearing a three piece tweed suit, the most brightly polished brown brogues she had ever seen, and carrying a walking stick topped with a bulldog's head cast in silver. Although his hair was white and his waistcoat covered a comfortable paunch, Susan was willing to bet he was fitter and stronger than many men of half his age.

"Thank you, Susie," he said, but instead of taking the doll, he stooped down and placing a large hand under Susan's scantily covered bottom, he lifted her up and carried her effortlessly over to the bed.

He sat down on the edge of the bed, with Susan sitting sideways on his left knee, and her legs dangling between his.

"Now, show me how you play with your dollies."

Susan looked at him from down-turned eyes, uncertain what to say. She was shaking like a leaf; wet between the legs and praying she wouldn't mark his suit. And now she could see her nipples, which couldn't have been any more prominent if she had painted them day-glo pink.

"Don't be shy of your Uncle Peter. That's silly." He discarded his cane and putting his thumb and finger under her chin, lifted her head. "We are going to be great friends, aren't we?"

Susan nodded. What else could she do?

"Good girl. Now you show me how you would undress this beautiful little lady ready for her bath."

Susan's eyes shot to his, and he nodded to show that she should do it, without any further delay. Susan started to undress the doll. It was one of the larger ones which was meant to represent a little girl of about twelve or thirteen, with very realistic looking light blue eyes and short golden hair like her own. And Susan knew she was also very realistic further down, with breasts which were ready for a training bra, and working genitalia. He insisted on Susan fetching the potty and showing him how it worked.

"Goodness me," he said, as the jet of water rattled into the plastic bowl, reminding Susan that she would like to go herself. "That's very realistic, isn't it?" Susan assumed his question was meant to be rhetorical, but he looked at her waiting for a reply.

Susan nodded, but still he waited.

"Yes, Uncle Peter," she said, accepting the inevitable.

"You know some people find that very erotic?"

She didn't and she wondered why they should, but she didn't want to discuss it with him.

"Yes, Uncle Peter."

"Show me again," he demanded, and when she looked uncomfortable, he laughed. "What's the matter, do you need to go yourself?"

"Yes, Uncle."

"Not to worry then, but can you hang on while I tell you what's happening?"

She didn't want to, she was already wriggling in discomfort and would soon have to clutch herself, but she did want to know what was happening, and she didn't want to cause him any annoyance.

"Yes, Uncle."

Susan put the doll and potty aside and sat on the carpet. She didn't want to go back and sit on his lap unless he insisted, but she was regretting choosing the baby-doll pyjamas. They were designed to make her look more provocative, not cover her modesty, which was why she had chosen them. But that was before she had known anyone other than her master would see her in them.

He smiled at her patiently waiting. She tried to pretend that she didn't understand what for, but he patted his knee and she knew that there was to be no escape. She wasn't sure which was worse anyway, having him stare at her blushing breasts, or having to sit on his knee feeling his closeness. She rose and reluctantly did as he wanted.

Now she knew, this was much worse. She couldn't help shuffling her bottom back and forth, changing from cheek to cheek and trying to ease her straining bladder. And each time that she wriggled he smiled at her indulgently, in an understanding manner.

"You know that your master is a writer?" Susan nodded. "Well he can only work in the mornings. Anything he writes in the afternoon is usually rubbish. Don't ask me why that is, he doesn't know himself. But it means that he normally works between six and noon, and no one must disturb him between those times. I'm staying with him for a few weeks, and there will only be the three of us here, so you will have to do all the housework on your own. There's nothing much really. Just the usual things, like cooking, washing and ironing, plus some light gardening to get you out in the fresh air. After he's finished work he will come down here to exercise, take a light meal, and a short nap, then the rest of his time is free. So normally you will see him in the afternoons and occasionally at night, if he's not entertaining, or going out. As I said, I will be around for a while, but you will hardly know I'm here. His routine and your duties are all written down."

"I see. Thank you, Uncle."

"Now, we need to get you sorted out before you burst." He laughed, his tone implying that she had been a little fidget, but very good under the circumstances.

He lifted her down. "Your master is working at the moment. Something he wants to get down before the muse escapes him. But as this is your first day, it's to be special. So once you're ready, I'm to take you up to his study and you can watch him work, until he's ready for you, OK?"

"Yes, Uncle."

"Come on then." He rose and she walked ahead of him into the bathroom.

"First of all, let's have you out of those nighties."

Susan had been expecting something like that to happen, but now it had, she was at a loss to know how to react. But he didn't give her a chance to be shy. He knelt down and slipped her top off.

"What a little beauty you are."

Now he made no pretence about looking at her and Susan was filled with emotions she didn't understand. She knew it was wrong. That there was something not nice about it. But what? If he wanted to pretend that she was a little girl, what harm did it do? Better that, than having him behave this way with real little girls. Lots of people role play, she told herself, but she knew it wasn't his behaviour she was finding so disturbing. It was her own. It was his fantasy they were enacting and there was no doubt that he was enjoying himself. But so was she. It was a shock to realise that, but true nevertheless. It was nice to have someone care about her. He was big and strong and kind. But he was also naughty. He wanted to be bad with her; do those things which an uncle and a niece shouldn't do together, and that made her body hum all over with tense excitement.

As his eyes continued to drink in her charms, making no pretence of how appealing he found her, she felt a stirring in her body and once more experienced a sensation which had laid dormant there for many years.

Like every other little girl, she had soon been made aware of the effect she had on grown men. Long before she was old enough to fully understand her true relationship to other people she was aware that there could be no such thing as a purely platonic relationship between heterosexual males and females. Nature isn't built that way. Perhaps, in the case of boys, it doesn't matter, but every little girl has to find this out for herself. Not that it's a burden. On the contrary, it's fun. An important part of the fun and excitement of growing up. But fraught with danger, especially for the men.

Most of the men she came in contact with were members of her own family. So it had been an incestuous game. And she was a precocious child who played it by sitting on their lap, giving them glimpses of her knickers: or best of all, letting her chosen favourite see her partly dressed.

There was no doubt that she was aware that what she was doing was wrong. And that any mistake could get the man in to serious trouble. So she had always been careful. Because she was in love. But whether with the man, or the game, she wasn't sure any more. There was no doubt that the game had such piquancy that after her first success, she was unable to restrain her need to try out her new found power.

When it is that a woman forgets about these experiences of her childhood, she wasn't sure. She had forgotten about them herself until now. And it was certain that, if her own mother's experiences had been similar to her own, she had forgotten about them by the time Susan was seven.

She could still remember the time on Southend beach when her mother was drying her in full view of Uncle Wilf. Susan had been aware that he was watching her, acutely aware of her naked body. But her mother had seen nothing amiss. In fact, she had asked Uncle Wilf to finish off while she went down to the sea and washed the sand out of Susan's bathing costume. Susan had felt Uncle Wilf's hands shaking through the towel and insisted he wipe between her legs.

Poor Uncle Wilf! When she had sat herself down on his lap, she had felt something else, and heard him groan. He had almost fled the moment her mother returned, and she could still hear her mother's concerned voice shouting after him: 'Are you alright, Wilf, you've gone quite white,' And Uncle Wilf had replied without looking back, murmuring something about a bad eel, but Susan had thought that he was probably getting confused between a bad eel and a nice snake. She had never quite forgotten that experience, but she had put it to the back of her mind; until now.

"Have you anything else to show me?"

Susan nodded, "Yes, Uncle."

Uncle Peter pulled her knickers down and Susan stepped out of them. He held them up so they could both see the damp patch.

"Oh dear." He looked at her and she blushed in shame.

Then he placed the pants aside and looked at her vulva for the first time. He continued to look at her for a very long time. And Susan watched him looking at her, enjoying the expression in his eyes, and the fact that he couldn't tear his gaze away from her. She knew then that she had wanted him to look at her all the time, from the very beginning, despite repeatedly telling herself that she didn't. It was wonderful to be stared at admiringly by a man like this. She didn't know why, but it was. It made her feel so proud and warm inside, and for the first time she felt a growing affection for her Uncle Peter.

"Turn round."

Susan did so and the sensation inside her was almost worse now, wondering what he was doing and thinking.

When she thought she would burst if he didn't say something he spoke at last. "You have the most beautiful little bum I have ever seen."

The palm of his hand caressed down the arch of her back and off the rise of her cheeks, launching itself from the smooth slope like Eddie The Eagle. It was the first time he had touched her naked flesh and her bottom twitched pleading for more. He placed the tips of his index fingers in the twin dimples at the bottom of her anal cheeks and she heard him chuckle.

"You are such a darling, you still have your baby dimples."

His examination was over. He placed his arm round her body, just below her breasts and gave her a couple of pats on her bottom.

"Now, miss, what are we to do about you wetting your pants, aye?"

Susan shuddered and her heart stood still. Uncle Peter's hand ran lightly over the cheeks of her bottom and she began to wriggle with anticipation.

"What do you think we should do, aye?" His voice, close to her ear, was thoughtful, as if he genuinely needed her advice.

"Please, Uncle, I deserve a smack."

"Yes, I think you do."

He bent her over his knee and she felt his large hand covering both cheeks of her bottom. He didn't keep her waiting. She felt his hand rise, and return again almost immediately, arriving back with a terrific crack which reverberated round and round the tiled room. The sensation was incredible. She had waited twenty-two years for that first smack, but it was worth it. It was wonderful. Just what she had always wanted. It was exactly what she deserved. Not for wetting her pants, but for making all those poor men wet theirs all those years ago. And best of all, now that it had arrived, she could be sure of herself at last, and what she wanted from life.

His hand rose and fell another five times. Until her bottom was red hot and she was whimpering with pleasure. It was perfect. Almost too perfect to bear. The heat and the pain, the humiliation and the wickedness, the retribution and forgiveness, and the love and understanding. They were what she had wanted all this time. And Uncle Peter would give them to her. He loved her enough to teach her how to be a good little girl.

She let the tears flow, and when he stood her upright again, she searched for his handsome face through eyes filled with shimmering liquid diamonds. He was pleased with her, his eyes told her that, and it was enough. She threw her arms round his neck and buried her face in his chest.

"There, there, little one, it's all over now."

He hugged her tight and patted her back. And she knew that she would always love this big kind bear of a man. She enjoyed her cuddle and didn't want it to end, but when he thought she had recovered enough, he wiped her eyes with a big white handkerchief and gave it to her to blow her nose on. She knew that she looked very serious. She couldn't help it. She was happier now than she had ever been. But it had been a traumatic experience and she still didn't fully understand. He kissed her eyes and tickled her tummy until she had to smile. Then he bent over her, and putting his lips against her shoulder at the base of her neck he blew a noisy wet raspberry. She screwed her shoulder up and squealed, trying to escape from him. But he took her under the arms, and lifting her up, swung her round and round with her feet off the ground making her squeal again until they were both laughing at her enjoyment of it.

For a moment the erotic spell was broken, but then he stopped her twirling and hugged her to him with his hand under her bottom. They were both still laughing, but now she put her arms round his neck and kissed him on the cheek. It was nice to be held in such strong capable arms with the rough material of his suit pressing into her skin and the musky tang of his aftershave filling her nostrils. She felt a stirring in her body again and his eyes followed hers to watch her nipples rise to their full height once more. He laughed, and, still holding her tight, he carried her over to the toilet and placed her down on it.

"Come on, show Uncle Peter what a big girl you are."

But of course, she couldn't.

"Do you want me to look away. Is that it?"

"Yes please, Uncle."

He turned away and as he went he stooped and picked up her night clothes. She tried to fill her mind with the least erotic thoughts she could find, and when she heard him closing the door of the washing machine on the other side of the partition, she at last felt able to go. Once she had started she couldn't stop. He came to the end of the partition and stood and looked at her. It had an effect on her which was similar to an orgasm. She opened her legs wider so that he could see a little better. She saw his slight nod of approval and almost shivered with a peculiar kind of pleasure. She had never known a man this well before. Even her father hadn't watched her pee once she had given up the potty. It was a private thing, especially for women. Yet this seemed so natural, as if there was no need for her to have any secrets from him. Not even secrets of the toilet. He moved towards her slowly, and as the stream of urine started to reduce, he stepped forward and tore a couple of sheets of toilet paper from the roll. When she had finished, she stood up and turned to him so that he could wipe her, and she walked off leaving him to dispose of the paper and flush it away.

Uncle Peter showed her how to use the enema and the douche and dried her with a bath sheet when she had showered.

"I'm sorry Uncle, I haven't any clothes, except a top coat, and I don't know where that is."

"Don't worry. You won't need any today and I shall buy you some for tomorrow. I know the sort of clothes the master will want you to wear and I will enjoy choosing them for you. Would you like that?"

"Yes please, Uncle."

"Good girl. Well we had better get you upstairs before he thinks I have run off with you." He knelt down again, putting his hands on her bottom. "Have you got a kiss for your old Uncle?"

Susan leant forward and taking his large head between her little hands, she kissed him on the lips. Then he took her up to her master's study.

Susan wasn't very good with heights and the narrow flight of stone steps which led up past the glass wall of the study scared her to death. On the open side, the vertical drop was only protected by an open iron handrail with an occasional vertical support and no spindles. Susan held on tight to the handrail and didn't dare look down. At the top there was a small stone landing which they entered through a door made of iron bars.

The side which bordered on the dungeon was also enclosed by iron bars, but on the other two sides, the walls were made of glass and looked in on three different rooms. Susan glimpsed a bedroom and a living room as she crossed over the landing and through the glass door into the study.

She looked back at the door she had entered by and it was no longer a door. On this side it was an oblong mirror in a gilt frame, in which she saw a naked young girl with a white face and an awed expression, clutching a large teddy bear under one arm.

CHAPTER 5

The door closed quietly behind Uncle Peter and Susan was alone with her master.

She turned to look at him.

She knew that whoever she met in future life there would never be a greater authority figure for her than this man. Her whole body was humming with fear and expectancy, as if it knew that she was in the presence of great danger. She longed for him to torture her, so that she could show her love for him, but at the same time she was terrified in case she should prove to be unworthy. Please, Lord, don't let me let him down. Don't let me be too weak or stupid. There was barely time for the silent prayer before he was speaking to her.

"Would you like to stand quietly and watch me work?" He placed his hands on her shoulders and she shuddered at the electricity of his touch.

"Yes please, Master." That was what she meant to say, but of coarse with her lisp and stutter, it actually came out as "Ye - ye - yeth please, Master."

He looked at her kindly, appreciating how difficult it was for her to overcome her stupid nervous affliction at moments of high tension.

"Who do we have here then?"

"Oscar, Master."

"Is he your special friend?"

"Yes, Master. He looks after me."

"Then we must find him somewhere suitable to sit where he can keep an eye on you."

He took the Teddy from her arms and crossed to a drinks table a few feet away. After a moment of trying, he managed to make Oscar comfortable, balanced on top of the shade of the large lamp which shared the table with several half filled decanters and an assortment of crystal glasses.

Susan watched him. She knew that he was trying to relax her. She hated her speech impediments. They had always held her back; making her too shy to speak. But she knew that this man would never tease her about them. He would be cruel to her and make her cry, but that would be her fault, because she loved and needed him so much.

"Is that alright?" He looked from Oscar to her.

She nodded her approval, but he pursed his lips and half raised one eyebrow.

"Yes. Thank you, Master."

He was prepared to forget her lisp, and wait patiently for her to control her stutter, but he wasn't going to excuse her altogether from speaking. She understood that, and it was as it should be. If only he didn't make her so nervous.

He walked over and stood in front of her again. He was looking at her breasts, totally absorbed in his own thoughts. She felt them going red. She could feel the heat in her neck and face as well and had no need to look in a mirror to remind herself how awful it made her look. Why did she have to be like this? She so wanted to please him; to appear cool, poised, and sophisticated. And instead she was glowing like a stop-light again. He closed his fists, then extending his bent index fingers, he ran their knuckles from just below her shoulders, and down to the rising mound of her breasts. They travelled smoothly up to the crests of her twin peaks, bumped over the cobble stones of her areolae, and came to rest against her nipples. And by the time they had completed their short journey, she was shuddering uncontrollably. She pressed her thighs together and struggled to

47

remain standing as her knees bent and her bottom dipped towards the floor.

He seemed not to notice the effect that his merest touch had on her. He turned away and walked back to his desk leaving her bent at the knees with her bum sticking out, struggling to cope with the wetness between her legs and the chaotic activity within her overworked loins which were continuing to make it worse.

"Come here."

He had the top right hand drawer of his desk open and she walked unsteadily over and stood beside him. He took out several beautiful leather straps and placed them on the top of the desk. They all had silver jewellery riveted to them. Most of them were about two inches wide, but one was longer than the others: and wider, about three inches. It was obviously a collar whereas the others were wrist and ankle straps.

On the inside, the leather was so soft that she longed to feel it caressing her throat. On the other side, the silver jewellery was so shockingly erotic and explicit that it made her blush again. But it was also so exquisitely made that she couldn't resist tracing some of the outlines with the tip of her index finger. Each piece of jewellery showed a different scene in which a young woman took part in sexual couplings with other creatures: men, women, animals, and half human monsters.

He took the collar from her shaking hands and she felt too embarrassed to meet his eyes. The message wasn't wasted on her. She had signed the contract. And all these perversions existed in the world. A woman's body could be used in all these different ways, by all these different creatures. Admittedly, she had signed the contract, willingly, but at the time she had had no idea that such perversions existed. That wasn't strictly true. Of course she had heard of such things, but she hadn't really believed that that was what he had in mind for her - had she?

The collar was very heavy and he fastened it very tightly, so that she could hardly swallow. He checked it by running his finger round inside it to demonstrate to them both that there was room for her to breath. It was so wide that she could no longer lower her chin and was forced to hold her head high. It was a strange combination, something between an animal's yoke, and a bejewelled choker for a princess. She knew that its beauty must enhance her own looks, but she was also aware that it turned her into a chattel, a thing he owned, his beautiful captive princess.

He was speaking again and demonstrating how spring clips and chains could be fitted to the hasps and rings which the jeweller had incorporated into the tableaux on the collar.

He fixed her wrist and ankle straps next. She could hardly breath now, and it had nothing to do with the restricting collar. He was turning her more and more into a slave with each new adornment which he fitted. The sensation in her very soul was almost unbelievable. She was no longer that stuttering, lisping, stumbling, red faced little girl who couldn't do anything right. She was an object of desire. His object, and his desire. Now she could do nothing wrong. She was his to use as he pleased. She no longer had any responsibility for herself. No blame: no shame: and no will, other than his. Each time his hands inadvertently touched her singing skin, or he stroked her arm or leg to check that the straps could move freely on them, she almost fainted with emotion.

He rose from fixing her last ankle strap and surveyed his work. His eyes dropped to her groin and she felt the embarrassment rise in her again. She could smell it herself and knew what he must be looking at. He ran his middle finger up her vaginal cleft, and when she recovered enough to stand almost upright again, he raised it so that she could see that it was wet with her juices. He took out a large white handkerchief, and flicking it open, wiped his finger.

"You're a good girl Susie. I'm very pleased with you."

He held her shoulders and kissed her lightly in the centre of her forehead.

"Come on."

He half supported her with a hand round her waist as he led her over to a heavy oak pillar which must have been at least eighteen inches thick. He stood her in front of it with her back to it, then rested her against it so that she could feel its hard surface against her bottom and shoulders. He fixed her wrists together in front of her before attaching them to a chain which ran through a ratchet high up on the pillar. Then he knelt and fixed her ankles to the very edges of the pillar so that her feet were about a foot-and-a-half apart. He stood again and smiled at her as he drew the chain through the ratchet.

Again his eyes reminded her of the watery sunshine of early Spring which is completely without warmth. What motivated him? Was it a strength, or a weakness? Did it drive him on as her own sexuality drove her? It didn't matter. Whatever the motive; fear, hate; inadequacy or dominance; it was all immaterial. He was going to hurt her. He was going to make her suffer for him. And that was what she wanted.

He continued to pull the chain through the ratchet until she was standing on tiptoe with her arms stretched above her head. At that point, other than the straps with their obscene imagery, she wore nothing. She was completely naked with her back arched and her breasts forced forward in a provocative manner which made her feel very beautiful and very wanton.

Now he held up - what? It was beautifully made, almost certainly by the same jeweller who had fashioned the straps.

Something about the way that he held it, draped in a curve between his hands, made her realise that it might be a bra.

But what a bra! It was made of sparkling silver with a cobweb of tiny chains forming each cup. She looked at him questioningly and he held it closer so that she could see the double headed serpent which linked the two cups. It was a dreadful beast with a fierce dragon's head at each end of its twisted body. Both of the mythical monster's open mouths were full of tiny teeth which lay exactly at the centre of the cups.

Even before he took one cup of the bra and placed his little finger through the hole in its centre, she had begun to guess the true nature of the garment, and imagine the pain that it must bring. He removed his finger, and pulled the top and bottom of the bra cup away from each other. The dragon's mouth must have been formed from a dozen unseen joints because it slowly moved to form a circle which shrank as the dragon closed its jaws. The space in the centre of the circle continued to reduce until the tiny teeth met and meshed together. Susan shuddered, her imagination making her anticipate the pain of them cutting in to her tender flesh. How ever painful a real serpent's bite, it couldn't possibly start to compare to this.

She was in ecstasy again, feeling him so close, filling her nostrils with the scent of his aftershave. She couldn't stop herself from groaning softly at the touch of his hands brushing tantalisingly against her burning flesh as he fitted each breast into its delicate cup. Her head was swimming now as he fixed one set of thin chains round her back, one round her neck, and the other over her shoulders. Then he took great care about positioning the cups and drawing the strings of the silver cobwebs tight so that they fitted snugly round each firm globe.

It was more than she could stand.

She closed her eyes and started to shudder as the orgasm consumed her. She couldn't have stopped herself however much her behaviour might have displeased him. But he didn't seem to mind, or even notice, as he continued to ensure that she was snugly encased within her silver chains. She longed to feel his lips pressing against hers, but she was aware that it was a forlorn hope. Someday, he might kiss her, and show her something more than sexual desire, but not now. For now she was only a slave who must serve him well and expect no reward. Slowly she overcame her emotion and recovered enough to open her eyes again.

He was holding a gag. She didn't want it. She could hardly breath already and she couldn't stand the thought of being further restricted. He saw the fear in her eyes as she shied away from him, trying to press the back of her head through the solid oak of the massive pillar. He waited for her patiently and after several swallows which still left her throat dry, she lowered her head and submitted. Once it was fitted he waited patiently again while she became accustomed to it. She bit into the plastic gum shield until her jaws ached. It made her feel better, and at last she recovered sufficiently to let him continue.

This time he held up a small plastic bowl with four equally spaced silver threads attached to its brim. At their other end they converged and were fixed to a small hook shaped like a woman's hand with long elegant fingers and pointed nails. She watched him fix the hook to the exact centre of the serpents body at the point where it spanned the deep cleft between her breasts. As he released the bowl, and its weight was taken by the monster's body, both sets of jaws closed until she could feel the first bite of the tiny teeth against the swollen flesh of her blood filled nipples.

Finally he attached a clear plastic bottle filled with water to an iron bracket above her head. He took one last look

52

at his preparations and without meeting her eyes, or saying anything, he retired behind his desk and started to work.

It didn't take long for Susan to discover how the torture worked. Once turned on end, the bottle slowly dripped water into a thimble-sized silver cup attached to its neck by a wire pivot. When the cup was full, the weight of the water made it tip over and release its liquid load into the bowl attached to the serpentine body. It may have been only a fluid ounce of water, but its weight was enough to make each dragons' jaw close a little more and bite a little harder into her flesh.

The cup pivoted back into position to catch the water from the dripping bottle once more, and the process started all over again. When it had happened eight times, she was in heaven. The pain was beautiful, and she was beautiful. The serpents' heads surrounded her nipples, and the thin silver chains imprisoned her breasts emphasizing their femininity. The wide collar held her head up high making her look proud and aloof, and the wrist and ankle straps now held her tight, making her young body appear vulnerable and available.

Only the area between her legs spoilt it for her. She could feel that her labia were curled right back allowing her vagina to swell out, and that her clitoris was thrusting forward like an erect penis. There was nothing childlike or pure about her nether regions now. There wasn't even anything delicate or feminine. It was only depraved and obscene, and she wished with all her heart that he had found some beautiful silver adornment for that part of her body, and then her happiness would have ben complete.

By the eleventh drop the pain was past pleasure. It filled her mind, numbing her brain. She was aware that he was still there, tapping away at his computer keyboard, as if he wasn't aware that she was even in the room with him, let alone in unbearable pain. Whenever she had sufficient strength, she opened her eyes, and looked at him through the pink mist which clouded her vision. She was sure that she had sensed him glance up on the last two occasions when the pivot had released its heavy load of water. Did it please him to see her throw her body around within the chafing straps and know that she was totally unable to make the slightest sound of protest?

She looked up in time to see another air bubble float lazily up to freedom in the top of the plastic bottle. It was as if it didn't have a care in the world. She closed her eyes as the pain bit in to her consciousness again. Was she still beautiful? Her eyes were tightly shut, and her forehead covered in beads of sweat and corrugated with lines of concentration as she struggled against the pain. Her mouth was hidden by the black leather gag, and her whole body flushed and wet.

And, what of that awful area between her legs, what must that look like? Her own juices were falling from her vagina to form a puddle on the polished planking at her feet. Each, drip, drip, drip, keeping time with the water seeping from the bottle above her head, like the constant ebbing away of her own life force.

The cup swivelled, the water fell, and the pain took over. For a moment she was completely incapable of all thought as she fought to control it. Then at last she shook it off and took another breath. The collar was so tight that every breath was a struggle now. The lack of air left her mind floating in a place she didn't recognise. She had been there before, and she knew she would go there again, but she didn't know where it was. She struggled to remember, but it didn't matter, it held no fear for her. It was only a vacuum full of peaceful white space where she could relax. But there was something else, something she was supposed to remember, and the white slowly turned pink and then red as she struggled to remember and surfaced back into a world full of reality and pain.

She managed to focus her eyes on the cup for a second and confirm her greatest dread. She must have passed out for a while. She knew that it took several minutes for the cup to fill, yet she could tell by the way it rocked and was turned to one side that already it was almost full with the next ounce of liquid. That would make thirteen. Unlucky thirteen. Would this be the one that broke her resolve? This time the sound in her screaming brain masked the awful plop of the new droplet joining the water already in the bowl.

That was the worst; the thirteenth drop. After that she almost resigned herself to losing her nipples, and her body seemed to release its own safety valve which made it completely incapable of registering any more pain. Her mind left her body and started floating a few feet overhead, becoming almost a disinterested spectator to their game.

The water dripped, and time passed. Somewhere the world continued and people went about their daily lives. Children laughed in the playground, women gossiped in the street, the traffic roared on the coast road as the distant cars chased each other's tails. But none of these sounds penetrated inside the quiet room to disturb its perfect silence.

The next drop would make sixteen. Was sixteen fluid ounces equal to one pound in weight? She had no idea. Her mother had never allowed her to share her kitchen. That was another area where she failed. She had no idea how to cook. A pound. It didn't sound a lot, but it was enough to make the pain numb every part of her body. And had it cost her her nipples? Would he allow the serpents jaws to amputate them? Or had they already been starved of blood for so long that they would die and drop off when he eventually released them?

God knew, she had complained about them often enough. But did she really want to lose them like this to prove her love? She hardly cared any more, that was a problem for the future, when she was still struggling with the present.

She heard the swivel turn in that deathly silent room, and knew that the sixteenth drop was on its way. This time she heard the plop of its arrival, and felt the jaws spring open. A fleeting thought raced in to light up her deadened brain. She needn't have worried about losing her nipples, the dragons' jaws were fitted with some sort of safety mechanism which made them spring open when they reached a certain tightness.

That was her last thought before merciful oblivion kidnapped her consciousness. Her body was suddenly filled with a white hot screaming pain, far more intense than anything she had experienced so far. She twisted in her bonds, screwing her body back and forth as if undergoing an electric shock. And the blood continued to force its way back into the tips of her deadened nipples stamping all over the sleeping nerves and kicking them back to life. And then with one last frantic jerk, she was still, with her body tipped forward, hanging heavily from the chain which held her wrists.

She opened her eyes and looked up into those deep dark mysterious pools. He must have carried her, because they were on the settee. How long she had been unconscious she didn't know. He must have undressed her too; if what she had been wearing could be considered to be clothing. The pain in her nipples was still unbearable. She doubted if it could have been any worse if someone had been burning them with a welding torch.

But it had been worth it to see that look in his eyes. She didn't want to risk annoying him, but she did so want a reward. He read her eyes and took pity on her. His hand brushed aside the damp hair on her forehead. Then his lips made their way down the bridge of her nose. Next they caressed her left eye, then her right. She held her breath and prayed. She lifted her face and opened her lips a little. But it wasn't to be. Not yet. She felt his palm stroking her cheek. Then it was on the back of her head, pulling her face against his chest. She held on to him for dear life and started to sob. His kindness had removed her resolve, and now she couldn't stop. She bit hard into his chest as he held her head and rocked her in his arms.

As her tears started to fade, he kissed her damp hair and his hand ran slowly down her spine to the cheeks of her bottom. It ran over her outer thighs, and as she opened her legs for him, it crossed over, and went inside to stroke up and down her inner thighs. It travelled lightly back and forth, over her bald vulva, up and down and round and round her legs, and in and out of the crack of her bum.

It stayed nowhere very long. And it didn't venture at all into the one area where she wanted it most. But nevertheless, her orgasm broke, and went on breaking, again and again, like a spitting volcano, as the pain of her recent torture and the ecstasy of his loving touch became mixed together in a confusing symphony in her exhausted brain. When, at long last, she was finally finished, he folded her in his arms and held her tight and safe while she drifted off to sleep.

When she awoke this time, she was still on the settee, with a couple of cushions under her head for pillows, and a blanket draped over her. She started to rise, but was very forcefully reminded of the state of her body. She felt as if she had been matched in a wrestling bout with a small bear: and lost.

She fell back against the cushions, but he must have heard her stir, because the next moment the sound of his two-fingered typing stopped. Every part of her body hurt. Her nipples were still the worst, but her stretched arms and legs were a close second, followed by her chafed wrists and ankles. She could have gone on and on mentally examining her poor body and finding one contender after another for the prize of most damaged part. But it was a nice pain. It was all over now. She had suffered and survived, and slowly her body would mend and make itself better. She opened her eyes and confirmed that he was crossing the room towards her.

"Stay where you are," he commanded kindly as she tried to rise again. "You've been very brave and I'm very pleased with you."

When he joined her on the settee he was still smiling and he brushed her unruly fringe from her forehead. Her hair was dry now she noted.

"Perhaps too brave." He turned back the top of the blanket and they both looked at her breasts. The pain in her nipples was only a dull throb now, and seemed considerably eased by his look of compassion. Each nipple had a few flakes of dead skin at the tip, and a dark ring where the monsters jaws had bitten into it.

"Oh, no, they're going to be alright," he said, airily. "I had forgotten that they were so big."

He saw her look and, misunderstanding it, tried to reassure her.

"Seriously. Don't worry, they'll soon be as good as new."

"But they will never be any smaller though, will they?"

"Smaller. Are you joking? They're beautiful. I have never seen anything more erotic, except your clit. You are a funny thing. You really think anyone would want them to be smaller?"

Susan nodded at him dumbly. It was like a scene from the Ugly Duckling. Could he really mean what he said?

He made as if to touch them with his lips and she drew in her breath and formed her own lips into a silent 'oooh' in anticipation of the pain.

"Perhaps not. But take my word for it. You couldn't have better tits or more gorgeous nipples. And the sight of your beautiful little cunt would be enough to make a sinner of the most devout saint."

They smiled at each other. She had never been this happy in her life before. She looked at her breasts with their damaged nipples and now she couldn't wait for them to be fully recovered and fat and long again. She wanted to carry on looking at them and remembering the kindest words that anyone had ever said to her, but he had lifted the blanket and was waiting to cover them over. He waited while she took a final adieu of them and smiled at her obvious joy as he tucked the blanket back in place. Now she desperately wanted him to hold her and kiss her. She looked pleadingly into his eyes and he kissed her on the forehead and the nose. It was nice, but it wasn't enough. He lifted her onto his knee and let the blanket slip from her body as he held her tight.

This was the most wonderful moment of her life. This man was more special to her than anyone in the world. He ought to be totally unobtainable. And she would have settled for that, and happily worshipped him from afar. But to actually have him cradle her in his arms, say that she was beautiful, and behave as if he was proud of her: that meant more than the world to her. Her toes curled up and her whole body melted as her love radiated out from deep within her. Her nipples rose at once and brushed painfully against his lambs-wool pullover. Her vagina became wet and burning hot, and she felt her labia unfurl again.

But it was no longer a feeling which filled her with shame. She had a lovely little cunt which was pretty enough to make the most devout saint sin. That was what he had said. She pushed with her muscles and her hips, opening it up even more and feeling her liberated clitoris stretch. She would never feel ashamed of her little cunny again, not now that she knew that her master loved it. He felt her desire and placed the palm of his hand on her cheek trying to calm her.

"My God, you're insatiable, aren't you?"

"As far as you're concerned, Master."

She pecked at his fingers, filling her eyes with desire for him, and at last he leant and gave her a fatherly peck on her dry lips.

"I can't deny you. No wonder Uncle Peter is besotted with you." He laughed at her look. "Yes we've been talking about you while you were asleep. He told me what a little charmer you are, and by God, he was right."

She continued to wiggle and squirm on his knee and he laughed at her antics and coaxed her to another orgasm which left her panting, breathless, and helplessly and eternally in love with him.

CHAPTER 6

"I'm going to beat you every day," he said. "There are some women that bring out the worst in me - nice innocent defenceless little girls like yourself. I think we have an opportunity here to train you to be something very special."

Susan noticed the bulge grow in his shorts as he spoke. Although his words made her tremble with fear, she wouldn't have had it any other way. He was her master and she was his slave to treat in any way he felt fit. And she would serve him faithfully and be grateful for any attention he paid her.

Without waiting for her, he turned on his heel and walked towards the dungeon.

Susan followed, looking across at Oscar as she passed him, almost envying the way that he sat safely on their little bed leaning back against the pillows. This was what she had wanted, but now that she was about to experience it, she was almost fainting with fear. She remembered how she had felt queuing up for her one and only ride on the Big Dipper. She had been so scared, but she had convinced herself that she would enjoy it really.. But she hadn't. Until then she hadn't known how scared of heights she really was, and it had been the most terrifying experience of her life. It had taught her not to rebel and sneak off to do what her mother had forbidden. What if this was the same? What if this was just pain and no enjoyment?

He stopped in front of what must be a flogging frame.

"This is where you will learn the most. But not yet. We must see how much you like the whip first."

He smiled at the obvious concern on her face.

"Don't worry, everyone likes the whip. It's just a matter of getting used to it so that it becomes an old friend. You enjoy it when you run don't you, even though your body is hurting?" He didn't wait for her reply. "This is the same, most of the time. It will make you feel alive, like you never have before."

He could see that she wasn't entirely convinced and her look of fear made him laugh.

"Yes, you're quite right. I'm not only going to tone you up and make you ready to enjoy your sex even more. I'm going to hurt you. There's nothing I can do about that. It's something I've got to have."

He didn't look sorry and Susan wondered if she would have to learn to be sorry for them both.

"Now, look at this beautiful virgin little botty." He turned her so that she could look at her bottom in one of the many mirrors. "Which whip would you choose for that?"

He took her over to the rack of whips and let her choose. Her finger traced along the row and she watched his reaction, hoping that his expression would give him away when she came to the right one. Finally her fingers closed around a long black carriage whip. He nodded and she pulled it free of the rack and handed it to him. He laughed, genuinely amused by her choice.

"No, I don't think so. That would slice our little bum into pieces. Look for something flat and wide."

She returned the carriage whip. Now that she knew what she was looking for she could see it at once. It was shaped like a small paddle made of stiff leather and it wasn't amongst the true whips at all, but hanging from a hook on the front of the rack. She was certain that that was the one which she should choose, but instead her fingers went to the one next to it. This one looked like a belt with a short handle and was made from a two inch wide strip of plaited leather. She lifted it from the hook and handed it to him. He took the handle in his right hand and ran his left hand up and down the plaited leather.

"Are you sure?" His eyebrows arched, emphasising the importance of the question.

She knew that it was the wrong choice for a novice, but now his question told her that it wasn't impossibly wrong.

"Yes, please, Master."

"Very well, come on."

She moved ahead of him, and he placed the whip over her shoulder so that it hung down on to her left breast. They continued like that, with Susan leading the way and her master using the whip to steer her to a leather vaulting horse. It was the sort with a hard leather body stuffed with horse hair, and a splayed leg at each corner which was adjustable for height by a wing bolt at the knee.

He bent her over it and adjusted it until she was standing on tip toe. Then he strapped her to it with her legs open wide. He showed her the flap of leather that she could grip between her teeth, then he ran his hands over her body, starting at her neck and ending at her ankles.

"Relax and enjoy it. You are about to be whipped by an expert. You will cry and scream and beg me to stop. You will think that you are going to die and wish that it was true. And you will come for me. You will come as you have never come before. There's no pleasure without pain, and you are about to discover how true that is."

He held the whip in front of her eyes. She looked at it properly for the first time and tried to imagine the plaited leather cutting in to her flesh. He saw her shudder with anticipation and placed his hand on her shoulder to calm her.

"Kiss it and beg it not to hurt you."

She did as he bid, her lips continually touching the leather as they moved in a silent prayer. He waited for her to finish, then removed it from sight.

"Beg me to beat you."

"Please, Master, I am a wicked unworthy girl. I have impure thoughts and I am full of vanity. Please beat me, Master, and show me the error of my ways."

She had no idea what he wanted, but her plea had come naturally and seemed to satisfy him. He made no comment, but he disappeared behind her and she waited for him to start. It seemed like an eternity until that first stroke hit her bottom and even then it brought nothing but pain. It hurt, but not so much that she couldn't endure it. But was that all? It wasn't until the sixth stroke, when she felt the first tear in her eye and the first stirring in her body. At first she was unsure what it meant, but it grew with each new stroke, and at last she was sure that there was a direct correlation between pain and sexual enjoyment for those who were brave enough to try it: or, at least, for her.

Each blow was to her bottom, but that wasn't where they had the greatest effect. With each new stroke she felt her breasts and vagina swelling more and more, as did her desire to scream with ecstasy.

Her great regret was that she couldn't see her breasts. They felt huge, with bullet hard nipples, and she was certain that they could never have looked better. Between every two or three blows he caressed her body with his hands and lips. His fingers always started at her shoulders and moved slowly down the contours of her body to the point where the last few blows had struck. They were firm and gentle and made her shudder. But they were as nothing compared to the effect of his lips, which traced along her spine and down in to the cleft between the cheeks of her bottom. They always left her shaking uncontrollably, unable to stop, until the next blow exploded on the stretched skin of her backside, and inside her head.

The need to scream was almost overwhelming now. Only the delay between each stroke allowed the passion and pain to recede enough to allow control to return to her brain. Then she was forced to wait, not knowing when the next touch of would come, or if it would be from the burning hot belt or his soft, soothing fingers. But she didn't scream, or cry out at all, until the tenth stroke, when he accidentally, or intentionally, covered the same spot as with the previous one and the pain was more than she could bear.

Now she felt other emotions: anger, hatred, and frustration. But only for a fleeting second. And when they were gone they were replaced with love. A love even greater than that which she had felt before. He had power over her. The power to hurt her. But she could calm that power. She could be submissive to his every wish, and then he wouldn't hurt her any more. He would protect her and keep her safe. And someday, he would love her in return. She needed to be free from her bonds, so that she could throw herself into his arms and hold him tight, feeling his inner calm quieting her shaking body. Then she wanted to feel him thrusting hard up inside her, beating her into submission.

His hands and lips were on her body again, and as they circled round and round her bottom, kissing and caressing away the fiery pain and leaving only the dull burning ache of frustration, she started to whimper, and then the flood gates opened and she started to cry, relieved to feel the tears tumbling down her cheeks.

He took a handful of her hair, and wrapping it round his fist, used it to raise her head. He wanted her to see that he had changed the instrument of torture for one which consisted of nine thin strips of knotted leather. She kissed it again and gave her silent prayer, and he took it away, ready to start. Now his blows were entirely different. He covered every part of her body without respite with a sharp stinging pain which was unrelenting and unbearable.

Susan screamed out with each new blow, and begged to be forgiven and released. She had never known such torment. She desperately searched for something which would stop him. She promised him anything he wanted; confessed to every imaginable sin; vowed to be good for all time. And finally, she simply begged for mercy, over and over again. But it was all to no avail, he was totally out of control and ignored every plea. And eventually she stopped screaming and crying out, and concentrated on surviving. She was too weak to scream any longer, or even cry. She desperately wished that she would soon be too weak to move as well, but it wasn't to be. Every touch of the whip made her jump and writhe within her bonds, filling every part of her body with pain. Her wrists and ankles burned from the straps. All her muscles, especially those in her stomach and thighs, ached from the constant movement. And her nipples, clitoris, and vagina, felt red raw from their constant pounding against the leather saddle of the vaulting horse.

She continued to bite on the leather strap, even though it had become slimy and filled her mouth with the unpleasant bitter taste of tannin. It mixed with the saltiness of the tears streaming from her eyes, and the two tastes combined to make her feel sick. The pain was too great now. The whole of her back, buttocks and thighs were on fire, and her head was swimming with confusion. She was convinced that he intended to kill her and she was becoming resigned to it. And then it stopped.

At first there was only the feeling of relief. Then as the pain receded she slowly became aware of the aroused condition of her body. Her mind was floating outside her body again, examining her state and imagining the condition of her body. It proceeded in a detached way, almost like a disinterested third party to the carnage which had taken place.

66

Her nipples were two hard metal studs which the firm leather of the vaulting horse was pressing back into the unyielding flesh of her breasts. The lips of her vagina had spread out in an attempt to swallow the body of the horse and were now firmly glued to its leather surface. Her whole body had blown up like a balloon, pulling her skin as tight as a drum and allowing her to feel the slightest movement of the smallest atom of air as it moved along its surface.

She had survived, but barely.

She was still in the centre of a fire which was searing her skin. And she desperately needed to be left alone for a few moments, so that she could learn to concentrate all her willpower on coping with the overwhelming flood of new messages which were screaming in from the damaged nerve ends in every part of her body.

He lifted her head again and showed her a thin wicked looking cane. Unable to speak, she tried to shake her head in disbelief. She had done her best, but she couldn't possibly take any more. Please, God, don't let him hurt me any more. But even as she prayed she knew that it would do no good.

The first stinging cut of the cane racked her with a pain which sliced through her body with a searing white heat. She came immediately then, with an intensity which made her terrified she would injure herself beyond repair.

She thrashed about within her bonds, grinding her hips against the padded saddle of the horse. She knew that her clitoris and nipples were much too delicate for the treatment which she was subjecting them to, but she had no choice, the sensation within them was too intense to be controlled in any other way.

Then she felt a new pain. The cane was in the cleft of her bottom with its point pressing hard into the dimpled flesh at the base of her right buttock. Her brain wanted to ignore it, but it wouldn't be denied. He increased the pressure until she thought that he would pierce the skin, and as he gained her attention, the sensations in her nipples and clitoris reduced to manageable levels. As her movements decreased, he removed the point from her flesh and turned the cane until its length lay vertically along her anal cleft. Suddenly she was sure that he intended to hit her there and she cried out in fear.

He moved the cane up and down within her cleft, like a bow on the strings of a violin. She realised that she was soaking wet with sweat. She could feel it moving between her skin and the polished surface of the cane. She began to relax. The sensation was enjoyable. It created an excitement deep inside her vagina, but it was also comforting. The cane continued to move up and down her cleft and each time that it pressed against her anal ring, she gave an involuntary jump, as the wonderful orgasmic mist spread to every area of her body.

He was playing her like an instrument now, and for the first time she realised that he had brought her body and mind to a level of perception far higher than anything she had experienced before. It was as if she had spent her life sitting on a high mountain peak surrounded by an impenetrable white mist, and now he had come along and blown the mist away, and set her free. She felt as free as a giant eagle, riding the thermal and looking down on the wonders of nature spread out below her, seeing everything with an eye which was trained to see the movement of God's smallest creatures.

She was approaching a climax again, and as she did so the inner walls of her vagina started to ripple, as if moving against an imaginary penis, the ring of her anus expanded and contracted, and her mouth opened in a silent scream. And as each of these orifices reacted at the same time, they all exuded fluid.

He was milking her dry. Despite the aching and soreness in every part of her body, and the knowledge that her suffering would be even worse when it was all over and she started to stiffen up, it was all worth while for these few moments of utter undiluted joy. This was the closest any human being could come to heaven on earth, she was sure of that. She was also sure that it couldn't possibly happen to many people. She had found the perfect lover. She adored him and he could make her come with a touch, or a kiss, and not many women could experience that. But this, this indescribable ecstasy, was out of this world and she wanted it to last for ever.

She was in a trance now, so wet that she couldn't believe that all of this liquid had come from her. He placed the cane sideways on her skin, in the arch of her back, and slid it smoothly up towards her shoulder blades, scraping the sweat before it. Then, with a flick of the wrist, he sent it flying off into space. It splattered on the stone floor like a sudden heavy fall of rain drops toppling from a leaf.

It was a slight relief, but more sweat was trickling down her body Her chin, breasts, and stomach, were all resting in puddles of their own. Beneath her thighs, the puddle was even worse. She hardly dared to think about what had caused it. It felt warm, and sticky, and, very, very, comforting.

At last the cane was gone and now it was only his hands cheek and lips which she felt caressing her body, coaxing it to more and more minor climaxes. He laid his head between her shoulder blades while his hands crept all over her body. She sighed and remembered to release the tongue of leather from between her teeth at last.

Now she was cool, and her body tingled with a new sensation as it realised that it was close to achieving what it desired most. In one direction his left hand caressed her face and breasts, while in the other, his right hand ran smoothly over her thighs and bottom. She pulled one of his fingers into her mouth and tried to hold it captive there, but as his lips travelled down her spine her mouth was forced open in a groan, and it escaped.

His left hand was beneath her hair, massaging her neck and shoulders, while his right hand explored the cleft of her bottom, her anus, and vagina, before sliding down behind her knees to her ankles.

She started to cry then. She wouldn't have believed that there could have been any more liquid left inside her, But there was. She lifted each foot in turn and screwed up her toes, trying to relieve the dull ache of longing which filled every part of her body. At least her body wasn't crying out to be penetrated any longer. It still shuddered in time with her sobs, but she knew that the end was in sight. His work was almost completed, and she would soon be more thoroughly shagged than any woman had been before. That would sound silly to most men, she thought. He hadn't entered her at all, and if she had been intact to begin with she would have remained clinically undefiled. But even so, they both knew that he had taken her more thoroughly than most women would ever be taken. He had taken, and she had given, on and on, until every part of her was his.

She had been in love with him from the very beginning, but now it was complete. He had beaten her, and abused her. He had caused her indescribable pain, to the point where she had almost prayed for death. But he had also cuddled, comforted, and protected her. And she worshipped him. He was her older brother, father, and God, all rolled into one. She wanted him to be her lover as well; of course she did. She wanted to give herself to him physically, and feel him deep inside her. But it didn't matter if he didn't want that. To feel him hold her in his arms. To have him cuddle her tight and kiss her. And most of all, to believe that he loved her. That would be sufficient, if that was all he felt able to give.

Chapter 7

When she awoke it was almost ten o'clock and already dark.
Her body had stiffened up, as she had known it would. She
made her way painfully to the bathroom and forced herself
to stand in the warm spray of the shower until she felt strong
enough to wash herself clean. Afterwards she felt much
better. She chose a new nightdress. It had a picture of Pooh
on it, looking down forlornly into an almost empty pot of
honey. It felt crisp and clean and smelt of the outdoors. It
reminded her of simpler childhood days and helped her to
forget her aches and pains. She stripped the bed and put on
nice crisp new sheets. Her new nightie was loose fitting
and meant to be worn without knickers, but where it did
touch her skin, especially on her nipples, the feel of the soft
cotton was a constant reminder of how sore she felt.

She thought about the bulge she had seen in her master's
shorts before he had beaten her. It had still been there afterwards, and just as big, with a large wet spot at its centre,
but he hadn't done anything about it.

She looked up towards the glass wall, as if doing so
would help her to read his mind. The curtains were closed
and the study was in darkness, but she could see a faint
light reflected in the plate glass. Immediately curious, and
clutching Oscar close to her chest, she stood up and walked
to the end of her mat, looking round into the darkness beyond. She had reached the end of her night time world, in
which she felt relatively safe. Beyond was the darkness and
the true dungeon, where anything might lurk in wait for
her, and where almost anything might happen.

But she had to be brave if she wanted to know what the light meant. She raced across the dark dungeon and mounted the steep stairs, trying not to think of the height. And presently she stood on the small landing looking into the brightly lit lounge. She suspected that the glass door she was looking through must be a mirror on its other side. But she couldn't be sure, so she stood where she was trying to stay out of sight in the darkness. There was obviously a party in full swing on the other side of the glass. She could hear muffled voices and music and see some people sitting talking and others moving in and out of her line of vision.

Suddenly a figure appeared from nowhere and stood in front of the glass door. Susan instinctively moved back into the shadows, almost losing her footing as she did so, and giving a little squeal. For a moment the woman stopped patting ineffectually at her hair and glanced to either side, as if trying to locate the source of the sound, but she dismissed it almost immediately and returned to preening herself.

Susan was now certain that she couldn't be seen. Emboldened, she stepped forward and amused herself by joining the woman on the other side of the glass in her minute inspection of herself. Not that the woman had much to worry about. There wasn't anything out of place, and she was gorgeous. Susan guessed at her place of origin as Singapore. She had long raven-black hair, which she was wearing pinned up, and beautiful blemish free olive skin. She had the most exquisite face that Susan had ever seen, with a long straight nose, deep brown oval eyes, thin cupid bow lips, and small even white teeth.

Her evening dress was so tight that it left no room for underwear. It was made of a fine soft silk which was moulded to her body and Susan fancied that she could even see the slight mound and dark shadow of her pubis through the thin material. It was ankle length, but split to the waist on the left side, and completely open at the top, leaving her shoulders and arms free without the use of straps.

Wearing such a dress was the closest possible thing to being undressed in public. And if it hadn't come from a top fashion house and cost a fortune, it might have been considered too daring.

And now the woman pulled it down off her breasts, until the top of her light brown areolae showed, then adjusted it back a fraction.

A man appeared by her side, holding two glasses of wine. Susan gasped - it was her master! Even though she knew that he couldn't see her she felt like averting her eyes. The woman turned and accepted one of the drinks from him. And as she did so, the glance which passed between them pierced Susan's heart like a dagger. They moved away, going further into the room. Susan's eyes followed their progress, but her mind was still locked on the vision of how the woman had accepted the glass. She saw every detail of her slender fingers with their long perfectly manicured pearl pink nails. She watched them touch the back of his hand and then run smoothly over the suntanned skin to the stem of the glass. She again felt the shock in her own groin at the intimate contact and imagined how wonderful it must be to have the confidence to touch a man in such a way. Especially a man such as her master.

No wonder he dressed Susan as a child and beat her. She could never hope to posses the confidence, poise, and beauty, to match such an assured, sophisticated, and sexy, woman.

The couple had stopped, near to the open doorway. They were still smiling at each other, with their eyes locked in mutual admiration as they chatted easily to each other. The woman lifted her arm and ran her hand up under the lapel of his white dinner jacket to rest on his shoulder at the base of his neck. This was too much for Susan. The woman might just as well tattoo a sign on her forehead saying: 'Please bonk me,' she thought. But she knew that she was wrong. The woman was using her charms to tease him in a socially acceptable way. Her actions merely said that he pleased her, not that she was definitely available. It was up to him to decide if he wanted to respond and try to come to some mutually acceptable arrangement.

Again Susan felt the sensation of inadequacy and despair. How had this woman learnt how to flirt so effortlessly and expertly? She had never done anything like that herself. But she could feel how exciting it must be. Her own body was tingling with the thrill of it and she was only a Peeping Tom who had no proper part in the proceedings. She would have gladly given anything to have even half this woman's knowledge and confidence. She really did know how to play grown-up's games.

The two lovers were still locked together. There was no doubt that the woman was perfect. She had her left side towards the room, and with the split in the dress wide open, Susan was having great difficulty in understanding what was preventing her from catching a fleeting glance of the woman's pubis. Susan looked at the other occupants of the room, and smiled. Apparently she wasn't the only one who was wrestling with that particular problem. Every man there was finding it difficult not to glance towards the courting couple each time that the woman laughed and arched her back, shifting her weight from one foot to the other. Surely, no one had the right to be that beautiful and happy?

Susan hated the bitch. She looked at her own reflection in the dark glass of the study door. She saw a small golden haired girl with drooping shoulders dangling a teddy bear by one paw so that one of his legs just touched the ground. She was dressed in a shapeless short nightshirt which reached half-way down her thighs. The low neckline meant that it barely covered her chest and the deep splits up either

74

side clearly showed that she wasn't wearing any knickers. It would be easy to take her for a child except for the effect on the thin clinging material of her full rounded breasts, erect nipples, and protruding bottom.

Susan turned back to the view in the lounge and continued to hate and envy the Asian woman. She had never owned a dress like that and was sure that she never would. What would be the point? She wouldn't have the courage to carry it off even if she did have the suitable occasion on which to wear it. Anyway, she could never have brought herself to pay that sort of money for a single dress. Not when other people were starving. Exactly how much 'that sort of money' was, she wasn't sure. Probably as much as she would be prepared to pay for a small family car.

She looked round at the other people in the room again. The Asian woman's dress wasn't out of place, nor her well groomed looks. The kind of looks only achievable by people who could afford the best clothes and the time and money to pamper themselves. She noticed something else as well. It wasn't only the men who were interested in the couple. The women were also constantly glancing over at them. How wonderful, to be the centre of attention, partnered by the most desirable man in the room.

Suddenly something was happening. Something the women had been expecting. A couple had arrived late and were talking to the host. He introduced them to his companion and as the two women kissed each other there was a slight tightening of the newcomers jaw. Susan immediately checked the reaction of the other women in the room and confirmed that she hadn't imagined it. So this was what the women had been waiting and watching for. There had been something between this new woman and Susan's master, and as far as the woman was concerned it wasn't over yet. Susan looked at the newly arrived man. He was almost certainly the woman's husband. And, from the way he was laughing and joking with her master, he had no inkling of the secret which was shared by everyone else in the room.

The players left the room and Susan considered returning for a dressing gown and a pair of slippers, but she was scared of crossing the dark dungeon. She was also scared of missing what would happen when they came back to this room. Not that she could avoid missing a lot of it anyway. The lounge was only one of the rooms in use.

Time passed. It was now almost half-past eleven, according to the large ormolu clock on the mantelpiece in the lounge, which meant that she had been standing here clutching Oscar for almost three-quarters of an hour. And in all that time she hadn't seen her master, the Asian woman, or the couple who had arrived late. Not that it wasn't interesting watching the others.

Ten minutes later her patience was rewarded when the bed room was momentarily illuminated by the light from the landing as someone opened the door and slipped inside. A moment later a lamp was switched on and Susan saw her master with the blonde woman who had been a latecomer to the party. They kissed, and as they did so he released the zip on the woman's dress. He stepped back, tearing his lips from hers, and as their bodies parted, her dress slipped gracefully to the floor.

The blonde wasn't wearing a bra and Susan gasped at the sight of the heavy generously rounded breasts, and near hour-glass figure. The blonde was left wearing a pair of high-cut, satin coloured, silk, bikini briefs, with matching suspender belt, white stockings and white hi-heeled ankle strap shoes.

He stood back to admire her, and nodded his approval. The blonde was unable to resist seeing for herself. She turned her back on him and looked into the mirror. Susan's heart dropped again. This was another very beautiful woman. She was in her late twenties with a full firm bosom and no excess fat. He took hold of her breasts from behind and pulled her close to him. The blonde arched her spine and bent her head back to rest on his shoulder. He lowered his head, and as his lips met hers, she swivelled round to insist on a full kiss.

Susan saw the woman's knees bend, and experienced second hand the passion which had inspired that reaction. He continued to kiss her as she sank to her knees. She began to pull at his belt, trying to feed it through his buckle, but he stopped her, and ended their kiss. The blonde looked up at him, wondering why. He smiled at her, reassuring her that nothing was wrong. Then, taking both her hands in his, he pulled her forward so that she was off balance. If he had released her then, she would have toppled forward, but he didn't. The far end of the dressing table rested against an oak pillar which helped support the roof, and he threaded her hands either side of this and secured them there with a length of cord.

Susan heard the blonde speak, but the sound was too muffled for her to discern what she said. She saw his lips move as he made some response, and at that point Susan's curiosity got the better of her. On a sudden impulse, she decided to take the opportunity to open the glass door a fraction while they were still fully engrossed with each other. She pushed at it gently, but nothing happened. She held the door and pulled it towards her then placed her foot against it at the bottom and prised it open with the pressure of her toes. There was an almost imperceptible click as the ball catch moved and the door opened a fraction. Neither of the room's occupants appeared to notice, but she would now be able to hear everything which happened.

"But why?" The blonde sounded more intrigued than alarmed.

"Shush, my love, all will become clear."

He collected the few ornaments from the top of the dressing table and dumped them in a chair. Then he went behind her and placing his arms round her waist encouraged her to rise from her knees. He helped her to shuffle sideways towards the wall and half lifted her onto the dressing table so that she was lying along it with her groin against its near edge. He quickly slipped her knickers off, opened her legs wide, and secured her ankles to the legs of the dressing table. The blonde wasn't tall and she had to stretch to enable her toes to reach the floor. But Susan was left with a distinct impression that it was no lucky chance that she fitted at all, and that it wasn't the first time that the dressing table had been utilised in such a way to support a woman's body.

Susan couldn't take her eyes from the other woman's bottom. It was beautifully rounded and firm with soft white flesh and a deep cleft between the cheeks. She could just see her swollen vulva and a tuft of blonde pubic hair between her wide open legs. She had an impression of stretched legs, shapely ankles and neat little feet encased in sheer white nylon stockings, but her hungry eyes were anxious to be elsewhere. They travelled over the curve of the blonde's bum and along her arched back towards the sweetly rounded shoulders. The centre two feet of the dressing table was six inches lower than its two ends and Susan could just see that this allowed the blonde's heavy breasts to hang down freely with only the enlarged nipples pressing against the table's hard polished surface.

Susan felt the excitement racing through her body. The blonde's enforced pose was at once both obscene and beautiful. Her fettered body was so voluptuous and vulnerable that there could be only one possible outcome, and Susan's own body ached with her desire to witness their anticipated lovemaking.

Susan was so engrossed in looking at the woman's body that she almost missed what he was doing. He must have slipped something into his captive's mouth, because the next moment, he was securing it with a gag which forced her teeth apart and circled her head. Susan was very familiar with the feel of that type of gag, and the sensation of helplessness that it engendered in its wearer.

For the first time the woman sensed that there was something wrong and started to panic. She struggled against her bonds, but she had left it far to late and now she couldn't even make much of a noise to indicate her lack of sympathy with his intentions. She soon realised the futility of her actions, and lay still, resolved to her fate. Until he showed her the riding crop he intended to beat her with. Now she shook her head from side to side, making a muffled screaming noise in her throat, and again pulling franticly at her fastenings. Suddenly something gave way and the dressing table started to move alarmingly as her frenzied movements almost shook it apart, but her tormentor merely laughed.

Susan could see the juices glistening in the other woman's vagina. She could plainly see every pore in the tightly stretched skin of her raised buttocks. And she could see her tightly pursed anal ring staring at her like a single accusing eye. It was so firmly closed that nothing could pass through it, but as he placed the riding crop, first on one protective cheek, and then the other, it appeared to wink at her, twice. His intention was obvious, to indicate to the blonde where the first two blows would fall, and his actions weren't wasted on her. Her legs flexed and straightened and Susan saw the flesh on her bottom become even firmer as she tensed herself in readiness. Susan fidgeted about on her own legs, taking her weight first on one and then the other. But, as he slowly raised the hand holding the riding crop, she became still, took a deep breath, and held it.

It cracked twice, like the sound of two pistol shots, as he brought it down hard on the top of the dressing table, once on either side of the blonde's bent body. The blonde jumped as if she had been struck. And Susan's fingers were suddenly inside her own vagina and she was struggling not to groan out loud. As he started to caress the other woman's body, Susan's finger found her clitoris and began the slow circular motion which could only lead to one satisfactory conclusion.

At that moment a man appeared, as if by magic. He was tall and handsome, and he looked very distinguished, despite being dressed only in boxer shorts and ankle socks. Uncle Peter! For some reason, despite his permanently fixed saintly smile of inner contentment, he seemed even more sinister at that moment than when she had first seen him. It was as if a dark cloud of menace had entered the room, and it made her shudder with dread and a strange excitement

Uncle Peter watched with obvious enjoyment while his friend continued to caress up and down the blonde's body leaving her shaking with desire. He rose from his task and the two men looked at the blonde's twitching bottom and smiled their agreement at one another. Her master went to the far end of the room where the blonde would be able to watch him undress. Her desire was evident and so great that she had some difficulty in keeping her head raised and her frustration under control as she watched him slowly disrobe. Then he was down to his underpants and Susan had no more time to spare for considering the blonde's reaction. He removed his pants and Susan sighed with longing. He had a good firm erection and a large shapely cock: her eyes never left it for a moment as he made his way back to the blonde's rear.

It was perfect. It was big and handsome and she longed to be allowed to caress it, or better still, feel it pushing the sides of her vagina apart as it entered her. At the thought, her fingers returned to her vulva immediately, and were soon inside her vagina playing the part of that beautiful looking penis.

He came to look at himself in the mirror. His face held a self-satisfied little grin. She assumed that his good humour indicated that he was as pleased as she was by the appearance of his manhood. But that wasn't the case at all. When she reluctantly tore her gaze away from it, and followed the direction of his eyes, she found that he had been studying something else entirely. His gaze was centred on the blonde's bottom which was still twitching uncontrollably in anticipation of what she was about to receive.

He turned, smiling to Uncle Peter, who once more nodded his approval. He took up his position behind the blonde and Susan had her first chance for a proper look at his firm tight buttocks. She groaned and brought her wet fingers onto her clitoris. She didn't know about the blonde, but she was sure that she wouldn't last very much longer herself. Already she could feel her climax approaching and still he wasn't ready to start. He waited patiently while the blonde adjusted her weight from one leg to the other and then he moved forward and placed his penis in the cleft of her bottom.

Susan sighed with relief, and her own bottom twitched, as if it was her own cheeks that the heavy knob was pressing against. She could tell from his movements that he was moving his member down the blonde's cleft until it reached the mouth of her vagina. She saw his buttocks clench. He moved forward. Then he rammed it home. The blonde's body went rigid for a moment and a very creditable scream issued from her nose. He was leaning right over her, with his body on top of hers, and pressed tightly against her. Susan could see his arms moving and imagine his fingers on her nipples, twisting and teasing them. Her ears were full of the sound of the blonde woman squealing down her nose, and the sound of the juices squelching in her own vagina as her frantic fingers whipped them in to cream.

After so much anticipation and waiting, it was all over within seconds. There were a dozen more violent thrusts, and then, with a final grunt, he came. So did the blonde. And so did Susan. For a moment there was complete silence. Then the blonde started to cry and the dressing table squeaked as he lifted his weight from her and went silently into the bathroom.

CHAPTER 8

The blonde was obviously lost in her own thoughts, still enjoying the after affects of her massive orgasm, and waiting to be released from her bonds. So it was almost comical to see her reaction to feeling the end of the riding crop placed between her shoulder-blades. Her whole body suddenly jerked back to life and she tried to swivel her head round to see what was happening.

But Uncle Peter had made sure that he was safely beyond her peripheral vision and she saw only the end of the crop, which he held out for the blonde's inspection. She turned her head away in disbelief, and Susan could see that every part of her body was tense with rejection. She didn't want this. She had been bound, frightened, fucked, and satisfied. Now she wanted control of her body returned to her, and to be left alone to come to terms with what she had already experienced.

The tip of the crop started its journey down the blonde's spine. She flinched occasionally, as if she was being annoyed by a persistent insect, but she managed to retain the stiffness in her body - until it entered her anal cleft. Susan felt the fluttering in her own body and realised that the blonde's efforts to resist were doomed to failure. The tip of the crop played with her anal ring for a few moments, stimulating it in to life like a cruel child teasing a Venus Fly Trap.

Then he stroked each cheek of her bottom with the edge of it, before returning it on its journey. This time its tip started from the crease just below her left buttock and travelled down her thigh, past the back of her knee, and finally, into the arch of her foot. It was obvious that the blonde was very ticklish and she started to jig about as he repeated the procedure on her right leg.

The skin on her bottom was vibrating now, like the surface of a trifle on a dinner trolley. Susan's eyes were glued to the scene, but her hands were free, and now her left hand disappeared under her night shirt and found her right nipple. It was rock hard. She shuddered with ecstasy and opened her legs to admit her right hand to make the short journey over her inner thigh to her vulva. On the other side of the glass, Uncle Peter used the end of the crop to peel back the blonde's labia and tease out the remainder of the spent seed. The majority had already slipped free and fallen to the bare polished boards, but he took his time to clean her out, then he used her inadequate knickers to wipe the crop, her vagina, and finally the floor.

Uncle Peter gave the blonde's backside two little taps, like a conductor calling an orchestra to order. Susan watched, frozen by a sensation she had never experienced before. She was filled with a terror which rooted her to the spot. She couldn't breath, she couldn't move, and she couldn't pull her eyes away from the soft naked flesh of that defenceless bottom.

And then Uncle Peter commenced the punishment.

Susan's brain refused to function properly as the smooth unblemished skin became disfigured by bright crimson slashes. She felt eternally thankful that it was the blonde's shaking body which was receiving such inhuman punishment, not her own. Her heart went out to the other woman and she wanted to turn away and pretend that the sight wasn't kindling unknown passions within her, but she couldn't. She had never felt this excited by anything before and in her heart she was willing Uncle Peter on, hoping that he would forget himself and become a black hearted beast capable of the vilest depravation.

After eight strokes he stopped, but the blonde's movements didn't. Every part of her body was moving. It was if a storm was raging under her skin causing the flesh to move of its own volition as some mystical force sent messages rippling through the length and breath of her quivering sweat soaked form. She was making a strange whining whistling noise with her nose and she was dry fucking the dressing table; beating at it with all the considerable force of her lust inflamed thighs. She was completely out of control now, whipped up into a frenzy of salacious passion, like a bitch on heat who must achieve satisfaction at all costs.

For Susan, the sight of the other woman thrashing wildly at her bonds consumed by raw primitive desire and totally oblivious to any harm she might do herself, fuelled her own licentious thoughts. It drained the colour from her face, and brought her to the very edge of her own orgasmic climax. Her eyes and head were full of only two things. One was the sight of the wicked red slashes on the quivering white cheeks of the blonde's backside. The other was the sparkling drops of love juice which sprayed down from her tight blonde curls onto those beautiful soft creamy white inner thighs each time she thrust her straining groin against the rickety frame of the protesting dressing table. Susan's own body was now so inflamed by her voyeurism that she knew she would come before her fingers could possibly reach her clitoris.

While Susan had been engrossed in watching the blonde trying to thrash herself to pieces against the edge of the dressing table, Uncle Peter had removed his underpants. Now he turned slightly towards the mirror and Susan saw his penis for the first time; and came at once. She hastily thrust her fingers deeper into her vagina, and masturbated with quick long strokes, glorying in the hot sticky mess and the sight of an object which for once was truly deserving of the description: 'weapon'.

Susan had no doubt that was the way that Uncle Peter referred to it in his own mind. He was a tall man, well over six foot, and with a big sixteen stone frame, so it wouldn't have been surprising if he also had a large cock to match. But God had gone one better when it came to this most vital part of his anatomy. In fact, he had gone several better, and given him a cock designed for a giant. But it wasn't only its size which made Susan shudder and filled her with dread. It was the chilling mind of the man who owned it.

Uncle Peter admired it in the mirror stroking it underneath with his right hand. It jerked at once, but it couldn't make itself any harder than it already was. It was so thick and long, Susan felt her excitement rising once more at the sight of it. She tried to convince herself that it wasn't much longer than her master's, but she knew that it was. It was also a lot thicker, which probably made it appear shorter than it actually was. It would make most men's penises look as if they belonged to a child. It nestled in a bush of pubic hair which was as snowy white as the hair on his head.

She had presumed that Uncle Peter's hair had once been fair and lost colour with old age, but now she could see that he was a platinum blond. He continued to stand absently stroking his penis, like a young boy with a pet mouse, while the two of them admired it from their respective sides of the glass. The glans was bright shiny purple, the main vein dark blue with blood, and his scrotum blown up in to a large balloon. It was a primeval power guided by a primitive mind, and it filled Susan with dread for the fate of the blonde. Even worse, she knew that the day would come when she would be in Uncle Peter's clutches, and he would contemplate his weapon and her body with the same calculated relish.

A small globule of clear glutinous liquid appeared in the single blind eye of his glans. Uncle Peter ignored it as he continued to watch the reflection of the blonde in the mirror. She was calmer now, almost under control after her beating. He took a last glance at himself and then his eyes rose and seemed to look straight into Susan's.

She shuddered, suddenly convinced that he could see through the mirror. She waited for him to snatch open the door and jerk her inside that terrible room. Her heart was in her mouth and she was petrified with fear. Slowly she realised that his eyes had turned inward, like those of a hunter savouring the moment before the kill, and she let out her breath and felt her heart start to beat again. How many times can a heart take a shock like that before it gives up the ghost? Not very many, the way she felt at the moment.

His expression of self satisfaction and inner calm didn't change, but after a moment more, a light in his eyes showed that he was ready. He turned and strode the single pace to the blonde, and placing his thumbs in the cleft of her bottom and his fingers on the cheeks, he pulled them hard apart. Then he moved forward until the knob of his penis was against the entrance to her anal passage.

The blonde suspected what was about to happen and she started to thrash around frantically. In comparison Uncle Peter was totally calm. His head was bent in concentration and the top part of his body was perfectly still. Only a slight movement in his buttocks indicated that he was rotating the tip of his penis against the entrance to her anus, waiting for it to open for him.

Susan watched in horror. She had never been penetrated anywhere other than the vagina, and never carried out fellatio. Now she was about to witness the rape of another woman who it was obvious was as ignorant of anal sex as she was herself. The very thought of it shocked her to the core. She was terrified, and prayed to God for some miracle to happen so that the blonde would escape this terrible crime.

With one thrust of his clenched buttocks, Uncle Peter took what remained of the blonde's virginity. She gave a nasal scream like an animal in agony. It chilled Susan's blood and she knew that it was a sound which would remain with her for ever, as would Uncle Peter's self-satisfied grunt.

They remained like that for almost a minute, with the blonde refusing to move. Then slowly she relaxed and allowed him in until he was all the way home. Several more seconds ticked by during which it appeared to Susan that nothing was happening, then she realised that the blonde's body was moving. Almost imperceptibly at first, but then growing in intensity by the second, her body started to shake. Susan remembered an occasion when she had been forced to speak in front of the whole school and her leg had begun to shake uncontrollably. That seemed to be what was happening to the blonde now.

As the blonde's emotion and trembling grew, Susan saw the movement in Uncle Peter's buttocks as he clenched them and then released them. She realised that he must be tensing and relaxing his penis inside the tight confines of the blonde's rectum, and she marvelled at how such a slight movement could be multiplied into the violent trembling that now racked the blonde's body.

Uncle Peter forced seven orgasm's from the blonde, during which Susan came three times herself. She was so dry and exhausted that she felt mentally drained and physically ill, and she wondered how much more the blonde could possibly take. Then, at last, he appeared to be ready to take his own final enjoyment of her. He withdrew his penis to the point where Susan could see the underside of its purple hood. Susan was sure that she couldn't masturbate again and she sat forward supporting her weight on one hand. Girding up his loins, he thrust his member back deep into the blonde's rectum. It was an angry shiny purple, slicked with juice, and so thick and long that it appeared like a conga eel slipping back into its home deep inside the pink coral rock.

The blonde cried out in agony, with the strangled squeal emanating from her nose. And she continued to do so again and again as he continued to thrust into her.

At first Uncle Peter was relatively gentle, and other than her cries, the blonde seemed totally unresponsive, feeling only pain. But eventually he awakened her desire again and started to thrust harder and deeper. As he did so, the blonde was forced to exaggerate her own movements so that her body would recoil against his thrusts and protect itself from the worst of the violent shock wave. Susan watched in fascination as the blonde's anal ring stretched and was pulled more than an inch from her body as it clung tenaciously to his retreating shaft. Then, each time, his shaft broke free and slid from between its clinging lips until she almost saw the base of his knob again before he reversed direction and folded it up like a concertina as he bore into her once more.

Soon, they were urging their bodies on, like athletes in a sprint, until they both came, together. They jerked uncontrollably against each other. At first Uncle Peter tried not to call out, but after snorting down his nose a couple of times, the emotion was too much for him and even he was forced to give a stifled scream. The blonde had no such inhibitions. She needed relief, and unable to scream through her mouth, she perfected a sound through her nose which was much more frightening.

They rode each other frantically, with the sound of the tortured joints of the dressing table adding to the general din as they threatened to shake it apart. They seemed like two wild animals, each refusing to give the other victory. Then Uncle Peter clasped on the blonde's back and within a few moments all movement had stopped. It was as if they had killed each other and there was barely a sound from the room; until Uncle Peter gasped for breath and Susan saw his back move as he filled his starving lungs with life giving air.

Susan breathed again herself then and gratefully removed her fingers from her own sore body. How they had got there, and when, she didn't know. And it was with some surprise that she realised that she had used them to give herself yet another climax. Almost in a trance, she wondered about the blonde's crushed body and her master's ruined antique dressing table. And she watched as Uncle Peter's limp penis slowly slipped free of its snug hiding place and deposited a large gob of semen on to the polished boards, with a satisfying splat.

Uncle Peter wiped his penis on the blonde's knickers, recovered his boxer shorts, and disappeared. The blonde was alone in the room now, but it was far from quiet. The air whistled in her nose as she struggled for breath. Her heaving chest wheezed, and the dressing table continued to creak under the weight of her body. Susan picked up Oscar and clutched him tightly to her chest. Having watched the blonde horse whipped and violently violated by two different men, she now felt embarrassed to watch her further distress. For some reason it seemed an even greater invasion of privacy. She must leave her in peace to recover her breath and composure.

Whatever had happened in that bedroom, the world went on regardless. She turned her attention to the happenings in the lounge while she waited for the blonde to recover. The blonde's husband was sitting on one of a pair of settees positioned to face each other in the centre of the room. He was laughing and joking with three other men; totally oblivi-

90

ous to what had just taken place behind his back, a few feet away on the other side of the wall.

After a few minutes her master emerged from the bathroom into the bedroom. He was fully dressed in his evening clothes again and he looked poised and cool. He took a silver pocket knife from his jacket and cut the blonde free of her bonds. As he released each one he massaged the affected wrist or ankle. Finally he removed the blonde's gag. She was completely free, but much too stiff to rise unaided.

"Did you enjoy that, my dear?"

"You know I did, you bastard."

"Which was best, the first or the second?"

"What does it matter?"

"Indulge me."

"You want me to say that I enjoyed the anal, don't you?"

"Well, you did say that you didn't have to try it to know that you wouldn't like it."

The blonde said nothing.

"Well?"

"I loved it, as you bloody well know."

"Better than the straight fuck?"

"Better than anything you've done before. There, I've said it. Satisfied. You were great, the best yet."

He laughed "Thank you, my love, that was all I wanted to hear."

"You black hearted bastard. I love you, you know."

He knew, and he continued to laugh at her as he switched off the lamp and left the room, locking the door behind him. The blonde started to cry. In other circumstances it would have made Susan feel sad to listen to a grown woman sobbing in the dark. But she knew that there was no need for pity. The blonde was indulging herself, crying out her frustration in loving a man who could treat her so heartlessly. She was feeling sorry for herself, but they both knew, that deep down, the blonde wasn't interested in any other sort of man. Neither of them were. After a few moments the muffled sobbing stopped and Susan heard the blonde fumbling for the light switch. The woman sat against the end of the dressing table just looking at herself in the mirror. What was she thinking? She had enjoyed good sex, and she had enjoyed a good cry. Now it was time to go back to her normal boring life as a loving wife.

The blonde took a few more moments to gather herself, then screwed up her nose and felt under her bottom. She lifted herself wearily from the dressing table and took a few painful steps over to the fine Persian Rug. She squatted down, and using her fingers to open her anal crack, deposited the remaining sperm on to the beautifully woven material. She found her knickers and registered their soggy condition with some surprise. Then she used them to wipe herself, thoroughly, before throwing them across the room. Almost immediately she thought better of it and retrieved them. She placed them between the pillows on the left side of the double bed, before returning the covers and smoothing them flat so that no one would know they had been disturbed.

Susan was shocked at what she had seen. And even more shocked at her own behaviour. She had lost her senses and become carried away. Instead of being horrified she had taken sexual gratification from what she had been witnessing. And now that it was over, she felt ashamed of herself.

Of course, her natural instinct was to feel sorry for the blonde. The two friends had duped her into thinking that she was to have sex with one man. And, in fact, she was still under the impression that she had. Also, from what had been said between them at the end, she had already turned down the idea of anal sex. And the fact that she had enjoyed it after all didn't make up for the fact that she had been tricked into it. All in all, there was no denying that the two friends had pulled a very devious trick and been very naughty boys. Still, she couldn't help smiling. The blonde had been up to no good herself; cuckolding her husband. So it could be argued that she had only got herself to blame. Well it could, if, like Susan, you were jealous of the fact that she had just made love to the man you loved.

The blonde approached the mirror, and for the second time that night Susan watched a woman minutely examining herself. Her movements were painful and unsteady, and Susan thought that she could detect more pain behind the bloodshot eyes, but all in all she seemed remarkably resilient for someone who had just endured such a traumatic experience. Even allowing for the mascara runs, the flushed sweaty skin, and the ruffled hair, this woman wasn't quite as good looking as the Asian woman. But there wasn't enough in it to matter if a man's preference was for blondes. And Susan suspected that her figure, although heavier and slightly older, was probably every bit as good.

Susan followed the other woman's eyes and inspected her heavy breasts, tight stomach, and pubic mound. The woman ran her fingers through her tight damp curls, then pulled a face again as they came away sticky. She turned, and twisting her neck, examined the angry red marks on the cheeks of her bottom. Her lips formed an 'O' as she saw the unsightly slashes and she gingerly inspected them with her fingers, but soon realised that it wasn't a clever thing to do. She winced at the pain and turned her attention to an examination of her anal ring. It was now far larger than before and puckered out like a half open flower. She touched it gently with her middle finger and instantly the partly furled lips drew back from it, but there was no obvious permanent damage.

Satisfied for now, the blonde finished her inspection of her body and, for the first time, appeared to notice the door she was standing next to. She ducked her head inside, pulled the light cord, and obviously satisfied that it was a bathroom, collected her dress and disappeared inside. Susan waited to hear the commotion when she found Uncle Peter hiding in there. But nothing happened, and she finally realised that the bathroom must have another door which led into the study.

With the bedroom now empty, Susan turned her attention back to the lounge. She was surprised to see her master sitting with the group on the settees, which now included the Asian woman as well as the blonde woman's husband. Uncle Peter was standing talking with a different group by the fireplace. If anyone had noticed their absence, or the blonde's continued absence, they gave no indication of it. Everyone seemed very relaxed and convivial without a care in the world.

Susan was further surprised to see that their escapade in the bedroom had taken a lot less time than she had thought. It wasn't even midnight. Even so, it was obvious that some of the guests had started to leave and those who would stay until much later, were starting to congregate in the lounge.

Susan almost missed the blonde's departure from the bedroom. For some reason she had expected her to take a last look in the mirror, switch off the dressing table lamp, or be forced to wait for someone to return and unlock the door. But none of these things happened. She walked straight from the bedroom and a moment later reappeared in the lounge. Uncle Peter was the first to notice her arrival. He immediately excused himself from the group he was with and went over and spoke to her. They walked together to the sideboard where he mixed her a drink and accepted her hand to kiss as reward for his efforts.

Uncle Peter was charming and the blonde was flattered by his attention, but it appeared obvious to Susan that she was totally oblivious to the fact that she had just shared an extremely intimate few minutes with him.

She excused herself with a dismissive smile, and after exchanging a few more pleasantries, wandered over to join her husband's group. Uncle Peter watched her retreating back. His eyes lingered on the cheeks of her bottom as they rose and fell inside her tight skirt, and his normal contented smile seemed to contain a little more self satisfied warmth than usual. He returned to his group, standing by the empty fireplace, and the blonde woman squeezed in next to her husband, facing Susan's master on the other settee. She put her arm through her husband's and took possession of his hand, entwining her slim fingers through his and admiring her own immaculately red polished nails. He smiled at her fondly, acknowledging her return and her obvious affection for him, but the conversation didn't pause and no one took any more notice of her. Except Susan and Uncle Peter. They were both still fascinated by the situation. He took a last lingering look at her with a wistful faraway look in his eyes, before turning his attention back once more to the conversation of his own group.

It was almost a minute before the blonde found the courage to raise her eyes to look at Susan's master. He saw her look and returned her gaze with a cool disinterested smile. It was polite, but it gave her nothing, and she lowered her eyes immediately. The man was a cold devious callus swine. Susan felt her own clitoris and nipples react, and breathed out with a loud sigh of heartfelt longing.

She would like to have stayed to see what happened, but she was cold and stiff now, and very tired. So, first making sure that Uncle Peter was still in the lounge, she made her way to the bottom of the steps, and after a moment to summon up her courage, raced back to the pool of yellow light and her own safe little island on the brightly coloured mat.

She still felt very nervous of Uncle Peter and when she had dried herself she changed her nightdress for a pair of pyjamas.

For some reason she felt safer in trousers. It was ridiculous really. She placed her hand on her vulva and stretched her finger and thumb apart so that she could clearly see the outline of her labia beneath. As if this flimsy material could possibly protect her from that formidable weapon of Uncle Peter's.

She looked up at the study and saw someone standing watching her through a chink in the curtains. At first she thought it must be her master. It was one of his rules that the study must be kept locked and no one else was aloud to enter it when he wasn't there. But then she realised that tonight's experiences had proved that that rule didn't apply to Uncle Peter. Her heart missed a beat and she suddenly went cold. There was no doubt who was standing there watching her so patiently, without the slightest movement.

She shuddered and turned away. She hugged Oscar to her breast and shuffled down under the bed clothes until only the very tip of her head was showing. One of these nights he would come for her. But please God, not tonight, she silently prayed. She put her thumb into her mouth and squeezed Oscar firmly between her thighs. And her wide blue eyes stared into the impenetrable darkness beneath the sheets as she watched visions of Uncle Peter with the blonde. As she did so, she repeated a silent prayer over and over again.

"Please, God, not me. Please, Lord, not tonight."

CHAPTER 9

Susan was on the wheel, her master close behind her. She had passed through the wall of pain long ago. Now her mind was controlled by the automatic pilot which excluded all extraneous thoughts and allowed her to concentrate on the simple procedure of placing one foot in front of the other, over and over again.

She had reached the hill of despair, where reality forced its way back into her consciousness, screaming at her that she was tearing her poor misused body apart, fibre by fibre. She faltered. She desperately wanted to give up. Her exhausted brain and body could take no more. Suddenly the red mists of dull aching pain were split apart by the crack of the whip and a blinding white flash. The searing heat rushed through her body as she once more experienced the sensation of a thousand razor blades slicing the flesh from her bottom. She sobbed aloud and stumbled forward, the shock of the pain driving the remaining air from her body.

She must give in. She couldn't possibly take any more. Her brain and her body were both screaming at her to give in. And she wanted to, more than anything else in the world. Except one thing. She couldn't let her master down. Whatever happened. She must hold on to that one thought. And drive herself towards it, as if it were the white dot of light at the end of the tunnel. Even though her thighs couldn't possibly make one more movement of her concrete encased legs. Even though her knees and ankles couldn't support her weight any more. And even though each breath was like taking a million particles of broken glass into her lungs.

She continued on for a few more wobbly steps. Except that it wasn't her any longer. Some other entity had taken over completely and was pushing her body forward by pure instinct each time it felt the lash of the whip.

Then it was all over, and she felt his strong arms lifting her down. Instantly, it was all worth while. She loved her life as slave to her master, and this was one of the parts which she loved the most. They clung together, master and slave, both hot and sweaty and bent at the waist, gasping for air, experiencing a few minutes of shared intimacy which meant the world to her. He had told her from the start that he enjoyed punishing young women; making them suffer and beg him for mercy. But now she knew that another of his pleasures came from looking after his body, exercising it, and keeping it at a level of fitness which made him feel good. So they had at least two things in common. And luckily, they were the two things which interested them both the most.

Susan recovered enough to look up at the study window, and sure enough, Uncle Peter was there, staring down at them. He had already admitted to her that, whenever he was at home during the time when they were exercising, he would never miss the sight of her being chased on the wheel by her master with a whip. She enjoyed it herself, more than she could say. And it did them both good, pushing them on to greater efforts.

To Uncle Peter, this was the grand finale of the exercise session, but not to Susan. It always left her master buoyed up, and as he placed his arm on her shoulder and guided her off towards the bathroom, he was laughing and chatting making her feel like the usually ignored sister who has been allowed into her older brother's privileged world as an equal for a few precious minutes.

She hated the cold plunge and rushed to peel off her sports bra, socks, and trainers, but he was expecting her

98

break for freedom, and catching her by the arm, he swung her round, and the next moment her giggles changed to screams as she disappeared beneath the surface of the icy water.

Although she had been his slave for less than a fortnight Susan had already become used to his routine and knew that she would be content for it to continue for ever. This was the part of his day that she thought of as her own. They exercised together and lunched together. And then, while they were relaxing after their meal, he would often read some of his morning's work to her and ask her opinion about it.

Afterwards he normally took a short nap, and when she woke him it was with her choice of whip and a request for him to discipline her. A request with which he was always pleased to comply. Not that she gave him any reason to punish her. Just the opposite in fact. She loved him so much that her whole life was dedicated to pleasing him. And she did please him. She was sure of that.

Now, as they sat at one end of the battered old refectory table in the kitchen, finishing their salad, she positively radiated health and glowed with happiness. She knew that she must be the luckiest girl alive to belong to this wonderfully exciting man, who beat her every day, and who made her dream the most incredibly erotic thoughts about what he would do to her one day.

Suddenly a bell rang out with an aggressive clatter, shattering her contented stupor and making her jump with fright.

"Don't panic." He laughed, looking at the bell rack above the door. "It's only someone at the front door."

Susan started to rise uncertainly, conscious of her nudity and the fact that her clothes were all in her room downstairs.

"No, don't worry, Uncle Peter will answer it." He consulted his watch. "She must be eager, she's a little early. You tidy up here and then go back to your room."

Susan's heart dropped, but he didn't appear to notice her disappointment. It was the worst possible news she could have received. Not only was her master taken from her, but he was going to spend his time with another woman. Susan sat staring at the empty doorway through which he had left her, letting the emotions of self-pity and hatred fight for supremacy within her.

Susan sat on the bed with Oscar clutched to her chest, staring into space. She was wearing one of the little-girlie party frocks which Uncle Peter had bought her. And nothing else. All the dresses he had chosen for her were so short that they didn't cover her adequately when she bent over, or sat down.

That was the whole point of them. It gave her every opportunity to play the precocious little child and behave provocatively. And she loved it, and never slipped out of character. Like now; her mind was elsewhere, idly wandering back and forth between two related problems. Wondering where they were, her master and the unknown woman: and wondering what she would do if she ever lost her master permanently. But even so, she was still aware of how she would look to a secret observer.

If Uncle Peter looked down on her now, from his perch in the study, he wouldn't be disappointed in her appearance. With her legs apart and Oscar clutched to her chest, she would look for all the world like a small child, deep in thought, and completely unselfconscious about showing her knickers. Except that Uncle Peter hadn't provided any knickers.

She wasn't sure what made her kneel on the pillows and look out of the little window. She loved that window.

The sun seemed to stream in through it for most of the day, bathing her little bed in its golden warmth. And even when the friendly sun wasn't actually shining, the curtains were so colourful and bright, it seemed as if it was. There were actually two windows, one which she saw from inside her dungeon, and one that everyone else saw from the outside of the mill.

The lower part of the room, up to just above the window, was walled with stone. Susan estimated the stone to be over eighteen inches thick. And a single opening had been made into which two very different windows had been set: one facing in and one facing out.

On her first day in the garden, Susan had made a bee-line for her little window so, that in future when she lay in her bed, she would be able to picture how her room looked from the outside. But her expedition of discovery had ended in disappointment. On that side of the mill, there was only one window set in to the stone below the white painted weatherboard. So, there was only one window which could possibly be hers. But it didn't look like hers. Apart from its curved top, it looked exactly like all the other windows which stared sightlessly in on her dingy dungeon. It had the same small square panes, divided by thin Georgian glazing bars, and covered in a thin film of grime. And it had the same soulless indifference for the small blond child-like creature in the little-girl party frock who stood staring at it like Alice contemplating the rabbit burrow.

And when she had picked her way between the shrubs and knelt down with her eye against the glass, her only sight of the dim interior had been a few abandoned cobwebs littered with the dried out empty body shells of the spider's long departed victims.

The Asian woman squealed again, and Susan realised that it must have been her voice or laughter which had alerted her to the fact that there was someone in the garden. She was on the three-seater hammock which hung from the large Bramley's apple tree in the centre of the lawn. And she was completely naked. Susan's heart dropped when she saw her. She was more beautiful than anything she had ever seen before. Who's qualified to say which creature is the most perfect of God's creations? The butterfly, the fawn, the newly born kitten? Surely, few people would choose the adult human form? Not unless they had been privileged to see this enchanting Asian beauty.

The sight of her took Susan's breath away. She had something of all the others; the butterfly, the fawn, and the kitten, and many, many, more. She was the personification of human female beauty. She was perfection in every way, in everything she was, and everything she did. She was incapable of making her face or body look ugly, or of making an ungraceful movement. She was light and music, and fun and happiness. And Susan realised that she found her sexually attractive. If she can do that to me, another woman, she thought, just think what affect she must have on men.

For the first time Susan thought she understood something of what it is that men find attractive about women. It wasn't just this girl's face and figure which were unbelievably gorgeous. It was the perfect unblemished olive skin, the laugh, the smile, and every movement she made. She was breathtaking, so sensual, so delicate, so vulnerable, and ultimately, so desirable. Every man who saw her must feel the overwhelming urge to posses her. Not in a passive way, as an equal, but in a fiercely jealous and dominant way, with an all consuming love which would force him to cage her and hide her away from envious eyes, so that she was his, and only his, to take out in very special moments, to fondle, kiss, and adore.

The Asian girl was being tickled by Susan's master and each time she wriggled or writhed, and giggled and laughed, Susan felt herself loving her a little more. And that made her hatred for her all the stronger. Susan felt the awakening in her vagina, and as it spread throughout her body, she tried to deny it. She looked at her master. He was so strong and handsome. His white polo shirt was almost dazzling in its brightness. It was moulded to the beautifully developed contours of his torso and enhanced the golden brown of his tan.

They made a perfect couple. Susan's heart dropped and she felt a hollow emptiness in her stomach. She let her eyes stray to the bulge in his blue cotton slacks, and felt a jolt of desire, and loss. But she knew that it wasn't the sight of her master's body which was filling her with hot longing. She allowed the jealousy and hatred to mix with her strange new lust, and slowly, her desire crept out from her vagina into every part of her body. It warmed her stomach and burned her breasts. It dried her throat and set up an ache deep within her anus. It turned her legs to jelly and curled her toes. And it called from within her clitoris making her fingers tremble with a deep need.

Help me, Oscar, she silently pleaded, and lifted the little bear up so that he too could peer over the window ledge at the cause of her anguish. He wanted to help her. To reassure her. But what could he do? He was a honest bear, and the Asian girl was the most beautiful creature on earth.

Susan watched in helpless silence as the scene in the garden continued to unfold.

Something was boring into Susan's back, forcing her to look back over her shoulder. She saw the still, silent, figure of Uncle Peter watching from the study. He seemed so distant and remote she could almost believe that he was a figment of her own imagination. The burning in her clitoris would be denied no longer. She lifted her dress at the front, pulling it forward and making sure that it also rose a little at the back. She trapped it between her thigh and Oscar's ample belly, making it look like an accident. Now she could

103

be sure that it was only half covering her posterior and that Uncle Peter would have a perfect view of the rounded cheeks of her little bare bum.

She dipped three fingers into her vagina to wet them with her oils. Then she used them to tease open the hood of her clitoris. She shuddered at the touch of a familiar friend as, at long last, she felt the soothing relief of her index finger pressing against her inflamed bud. She continued to look at Uncle Peter for a few moments longer. His expression didn't change, but she was sure she was doing what he wanted. Her eyes became misty and lost focus as the repetitive revolving movement of her finger worked its hypnotic magic.

She turned back to the scene in the garden. Her master was chasing the Asian girl round the lawn. She was much too fast and agile for him to catch; dodging and weaving, and placing herself just beyond his grasp, so that time and again his fingers ran over her smooth body without finding a grip. She was laughing and shrieking, happy in the knowledge that very soon she would allow him to catch her.

And eventually, when she did so, he punished her by tickling her into helpless submission, before lifting her effortlessly into his arms and carrying her over to the wooden picnic table.

He laid her down on her back on the teak table top, and then reaching up, pulled down two ropes from the branch of the apple tree and placed one ready formed noose over each ankle. The girl had recovered sufficiently to wonder what was happening now, and Susan heard him speak to her, no doubt warning her not to struggle, as he pulled on the ropes. Slowly he lifted her up on to her shoulders, her head, and finally, completely free of the table, so that she swung head down from the tree.

The girl swung gently back and forth on the ropes. Her legs were held open wide, facing full on to Susan. And even in this position, with gravity having a reverse affect on her body, she was still the most beautiful creature imaginable. Susan's eyes travelled slowly down from her elegant ankles along the long slender legs, to the apex of their join. The raven-black hair on her vulva had been partly removed so that although her pubic mound was thickly covered, her delicate pink lips were completely exposed and screaming out to be kissed.

Susan's eyes travelled on, over the slight rise of her belly, past the pierced belly button, to the two golden orbs, each with its small brown aureola and thrusting swollen nipple. At last Susan's gaze settled on the large brown upside down accusing eyes of the girl, and she felt ashamed. How could her master possibly look on those eyes and not release her at once, and beg for forgiveness? How could he possibly use such a beautiful creature so badly? Why didn't he rush to take her down and cuddle her in his arms, and beg her for forgiveness and to allow him to protect her from all the evil of the world?

Her master passed the twin ropes under a thick exposed root, which had long ago pushed its way through the turf of the lawn. He tied them off with the easy familiarity of the weekend yachtsman. He dragged the heavy table out of the way, then stood in front of her, measuring himself against her. He released the ropes and lowered her a little before tying them off again.

Now he stood in front of her again, and, obviously satisfied that she was now at the desired height, he dropped to his knees and released the girl's hair. After a moment of persuasion, it fell free and unwound until the very tip of it just touched the ground. Susan gasped in admiration. It was so thick and shiny and full of health. In her normal upright position it must hang down to her bottom and be thick enough to completely hide her body from the rear.

Susan's master stood, and, starting at the ankles, ran his hands all over that beautiful smooth olive skin, letting them linger on every contour and in every nook and cranny. Susan watched the girl's eyes, and as the dark lids flickered and closed, she tried to imagine what the girl was experiencing. He hitched up his trousers and casually placing his hands in his pockets, stood nonchalantly watching as the girl fought the fires which he had set raging beneath that wonderfully glowing golden skin. When her eyes opened again, they were wet and misty, and contained a contempt for her own weakness along with accusation and hatred for her tormentor.

He leant forward, and without removing his hands from his pockets, kissed her between the legs. The girl started to jiggle about at his first touch and as his lips and tongue continued their work, she tried to take him in her arms. But whether to push him from her, or pull him to her, wasn't certain, because he laughed and stood aside beyond her reach. He disappeared out of sight behind the tree for a moment and returned with two iron weights, like those used on old fashioned scales, and used them with short ropes to secure her arms so that they were spread as wide as her legs.

The girl started to plead with him now. Susan couldn't hear every word, but she knew that she was telling him that she felt ill and that he must let her down. He walked behind her again, where she couldn't see him, and Susan saw her look of anger change to one of despair as she realised that he intended to ignore her wishes and do just as he pleased.

Her master took his time walking over to a large willow tree which dominated one of the mixed borders full of shrubs and summer flowers. Taking a small knife from his pocket, he chose a branch and cut it free. He held it in his right hand and swished it backwards and forwards a few times to make sure it was supple enough for his purpose. Satisfied, he closed the knife and returned it to his pocket. He started back towards the apple tree and as he walked he carefully stripped the branch in an exaggerated fashion, playing a game of 'she loves me, she loves me not'.

The Asian girl had twisted round in her bonds, anxious to see him as soon as he came back into her line of vision. When she saw what he was doing, she must have immediately understood something which Susan did not, because she started franticly struggling against her restraining ropes. He stood in front of her and finished his game with the leaves. He was teasing her with it, smiling at her distress. The poor girl was shouting at him again; demanding and pleading. But Susan was in no doubt that she knew that it would do no good.

He tore the last leaf from the branch and held it up for her to see. He said something to her quietly which Susan couldn't hear. Not that she needed to. It was quite clear that the game was over and the decision had gone against the girl's wishes. He released his finger and thumb and the leaf spiralled slowly to the floor. They all watched it; all the way down until it landed lightly on the short grass.

The branch was completely bare of leaves now. He held it in his left hand and ran the fingers and thumb of his right hand along it, stopping every now and then to remove a discovered protuberances from it. Finally satisfied, he transferred it to his right hand and brought it down with an experimental swipe at the empty air. Susan gasped. Her suspicions were at last confirmed; it was an improvised whip.

The Asian girl started to scream at him with renewed vigour, struggling within her bonds, desperate to break free. But her eyes weren't so defiant now, and Susan suspected that she knew why.

She peered hard at the other girl's face feeling a heightening of her own sexual desire as she struggled to understand what lay behind her tortured expression. This girl was different to her. She didn't appear to be a natural submissive. He and she might be role playing, but Susan didn't think so. It was all too real. She was prepared to bet that the girl hadn't willingly given herself up to be punished.

But there was something in her manner which gave her true feelings away. She wasn't protesting as passionately as she should be. Why? If she really didn't want this to happen she should be moving heaven and earth to convince him that he mustn't do it. But she was holding back. And Susan suspected that it was because she was curious to know the answer to the question which must torment every woman. Susan had come to realise that it had certainly tormented her, practically from her very first day as a little girl, when she had taken her first stumbling steps out into the wider world. She had heard other woman say that it was something which they had never thought about. But if that was so, why were they so much on the defensive? Why did they behave as if they were at war with the male sex, fighting to recapture the status which was rightfully theirs? In Susan's opinion there could be only one reason. Because they felt a primal urge deep inside them. The urge to submit; to allow themselves to be dominated by a superior force.

What would it be like to be dominated and humiliated by a man? A man who was like Daddy, or her favourite teacher, but who was also her lover? How would it feel to be bound and helpless, and totally in his power? Were those the questions this Asian beauty was asking herself now? This girl was no feminist. She admired men and desired their love. And she was an intelligent woman who would be curious to know the truth about her own sexuality.

Susan could imagine the turmoil in her mind as she struggled to come to terms with what was about to happen to her. How did she know that she wouldn't like it unless she tried it? Surely it was better to reject a thing from knowledge, than from ignorance? But what if she didn't want to reject it? What if she liked it? What then? Women were different to men. Not superior; not inferior; just different. But if she allowed herself to submit to his will, and allowed him to beat her, wouldn't that make her inferior to him? And wouldn't that be wrong, however much she enjoyed it?

Susan would never know for sure what the true arguments were which were going on in the other girl's head, but they didn't matter anyway. She had already made up her mind. Curiosity had won again. She had the opportunity to find out about herself and it was easier to let it happen than to try to fight it. She might never have this chance again. How could she possibly deny herself? And once it was all over, if the truth was too traumatic to accept, she had a ready made scapegoat. It wasn't her fault; she had been forced to submit to it against her will.

Susan's own emotions were in turmoil now. She felt jealousy, and hatred, and a strange exhilaration at the knowledge that her master was about to brutalise and defile this alluring and defenceless little creature. To break her, as a spiteful child might break a butterfly's wing. She felt the blood lust of the public execution; the wickedness of her part as a voyeuse.

She felt the excitement of knowing that Uncle Peter was watching her with a mistaken lust for a child's body. She felt love and desire, and the longing to feel her own pain and humiliation. She felt so many different things; so many different emotions which she had never felt before. And they were all mixed together, coursing through her body like a wild stampede that made her feel tight and faint. She could hardly breath, and the tension inside her head made it feel as if it was being constricted within a tightening metal band.

Susan's master rolled the branch up until it formed a ring the size of a large dinner plate. Then he pulled it and contracted it until it was down to the size of a saucer. Satisfied at last, he uncoiled it, gave a couple of flicks with his wrists to test its suppleness. Then moved to the side of his victim. Susan watched spellbound. The Asian girl's eyes were tightly closed now as she waited to feel the first lash of his whip. What would it do to her body? What would it do to her mind? How would she cope with the pain, and the humiliation? Could she still remain free, a highly intelligent and educated human being? Or would that first blow enslave her, and turn her back into a primitive animal?

Susan waited with bated breath. But her master was in no hurry. He took his time, taking a couple of slow practice swings and watching the tip of the improvised whip draw a crescent in the air a few feet above the perfectly manicured lawn. Then, at the limit of the third swing his body twisted swiftly back towards his victim. Using all the power of his hips, shoulder, and arm he brought the first blow singing through the air to land like the crack of doom on the tight olive skin of her sweetly rounded buttocks.

Susan's scream blocked out the Asian girl's own terrible cry and by the time she opened her eyes the second stroke was already on its way. This time she was unable to force her staring eyes to close. The end of the whippy branch coiled round the young girl's body striking the front of her thighs, making her scream out again in terror and agony. Susan looked in horror at the girl's bulging eyes and the knotted veins on her neck and forehead. And almost in a dream she heard the crack of the willow as the third stroke scored across the beautiful body.

Each blow sounded loud enough to be inside the room. The girl's terrified screams filled Susan's head. She put her hands to her ears, but she couldn't block them out. And neither could she turn away. She watched the beautiful body jump within its tethers, twisting and turning this way and that in a crazy disjointed fashion as it danced to his awful tune. It was terrifying, like watching a brutal murder conducted with a terrible psychopathic violence which went on and on without end.

Susan knew that Uncle Peter had come to stand behind her, watching the same dreadful scene, but he didn't speak and she didn't turn round. Outside in the garden, her master finished his vile work and let his whip-arm fall to his side. The girl continued to move for a moment, like a cork bobbing in a current. Then she hung limply from the ropes, all resistance beaten from her. Her body glistened with a faint mist of sweat which made it glow like oiled gold. It covered the beautiful olive skin and it twinkled in her pubic hair, like tiny pearls on a raven's wing.

Her master waited patiently to recover his breath. And all the time the terrible black violence could be seen rising in him again. When he was ready he went to stand in front of the poor beaten girl, and took up position with his legs wide apart. Sensing him there she opened her eyes and looked up into his face. Those wide olive eyes were full of fear, terror, and pleading. She had endured enough. There was no need for any more. She would never defy him or deny him anything. Susan loved him to desperation, but she wanted to scream at him - to tell him that it was too much. He must cut her down, hug her, love her, and make her better.

Her master flicked the whip so that it sailed up between the Asian beauty's wide open legs and came to rest on the precious jewel at their join. The terrified girl's eyes opened wider, until Susan felt sure that they must bulge from their sockets. And she knew that her own eyes must look the same. His intention was clear. But neither of them could believe that he would really do it...

The Asian girl did. Her eyes were screwed up tight and her whole body trembled as she hung there, waiting.

He was in no hurry.

He strolled over to the tree and cut another small branch, trimmed it down. When he touched her with it she jumped as if it was electrified. Her eyes were still tightly closed. She did not realise he was going to beat her with something so much lighter.

Lighter, but still effective, though it would do no permanent damage.

Now his arm was raised, and Susan closed her eyes also. She heard the swish and the strike and opened them again for long enough to see the helpless girl twisting and turning in her bonds, desperately trying to drive the unbearable pain out of her body. And all the time the girl's scream went on and on like a never ending nightmare which filled Susan's head, driving out all cohesive thought. And finally she saw his arm raised again before she closed her eyes for the final time. And kept them closed while the terrible sounds continued and her own hot tears poured from between her lids and went coursing down her cheeks to drip from her shaking chin.

When all sound ceased, she lifted her head and opened her eyes again. Once more she looked out on that dreadful scene. Through her streaming tears she made out the wobbly image of the Asian girl. She looked so small and humble as if she had found some way of drawing her body back within itself. Her tear stained face was empty of all expression as if the mind behind it had suffered an experience too traumatic to comprehend. Susan's master was standing behind her now, the whip discarded beside him on the grass. But it was easy for Susan to understand what had happened. His raging sexual insanity had forced him to administer two blows between his victims legs from the front, and then walk round her and administer two more from the rear.

112

And all the time, while this was going on, he had listened to the poor girl's cries for mercy and witnessed her unbearable pain. How could he? What sort of monster was he? And what sort of vile creature was she to still love and worship him?

Her master once more walked slowly round until he was standing in front of the Asian girl. Then, just as unhurriedly he pulled off his polo shirt and dropped it on the grass. Just as carefully, he removed his trousers and placed them on the shirt.

The girl opened her eyes as he pushed his boxer shorts down and stepped out of them. Immediately her eyes recovered their sparkle and lit up with desire. Susan saw her swallow, as her parched mouth filled with saliva once more. There was no hesitation, as he stepped forward, she took him eagerly into her mouth. There was also no hesitation on his part. He placed his hands behind her head and rammed his cock deep into her throat. Susan gasped in horror, imagining how it must feel to have a man's manhood thrust deep inside your throat cutting off the air. She saw the muscles straining in his, back, shoulders, and arms, and knew that he was holding her still, calming her, and forcing her to learn how to breath and not to wretch. At last the tension went from her body as once more she was forced to submit. Then he started to fuck her with long hard strokes.

Susan felt Uncle Peter's hand on her bottom, but she didn't pause in her frantic manipulation of her clitoris. He fondled each cheek and she felt the electricity of his excitement. Out in the garden her master paused for a few moments, and bent and placed his head between the girl's legs, joining his sweet lips to her inflamed labia. Uncle Peter's fingers entered Susan's vagina, making her shudder, and breaking her rhythm on her clitoris. Her muscles tightened eagerly round them, begging them to stay and join her in her frenzied attack on her own body.

113

The girl's legs stretched and her toes furled and un-furled continuously as she tried to obtain some relief from her master's probing tongue. Uncle Peter's fingers, thick with Susan's juices, worried and teased the entrance to her anal passage, which she instinctively closed against him. She knew that she couldn't delay much longer and she willed her master on, silently urging him to end it. And then his hips were moving backwards and forwards again and his buttocks contracting and releasing as he thrust in to the Asian girl's throat.

Uncle Peter's index finger entered Susan's anal passage and she squealed, alarmed at a sensation she had never experienced before. She didn't want him in there and she tried to force him out, but her master had lifted his head from the other girl's vagina and was about to come. With a bellow he did so, contracting his buttocks and thrusting the full length of his shaft into the girl's throat. She went in-sane, thrashing about on the ropes as the orgasm took her. And his sperm descended her nostrils, forcing her to panic in her fight for air. And as Uncle Peter's finger entered all the way in to Susan's anus and she felt his knuckles press-ing hard in to the soft flesh of her bum, she exploded and marvelled at an orgasm that turned her entire body to jelly, making her release Oscar and fall forward with her fore-head against the cool glass of the window.

Long after she could no longer bear to touch her clito-ris, Uncle Peter's finger moved inside her, and she listened to the squelching of her juices and wondered how her body had produced so much. It was nice after all. Uncle Peter was big and strong and gentle. And she had been wrong to be scared of him and to have dreaded this moment. It was lovely. He seemed to know what her body wanted and be able to give her one long orgasm, letting her float in a gen-tly rocking sea of never ending passion.

Slowly the motion of his finger decreased and finally stopped, remaining inside her, as comforting as she found the thumb in her mouth to be at night time. When she was ready, he withdrew his finger and she turned to him and buried her head in his shoulder. He lifted her with his hands under her bottom, and rocked her gently back and forth until she drifted off to sleep.

CHAPTER 10

"You're my very favourite uncle in all the world, Uncle Peter."

"Thank you and you're my favourite little niece, who I want to spoil to death. Come and see what I've bought you."

He carried her the few feet to the end of the mat where something was hidden under a striped sheet. Even with the cover over it, it was obvious what it was. He unveiled it without further ado and revealed a large wooden rocking horse. It was the type with a flat stand, on top of which a brightly varnished horse's body moves back and forth. The horse was a Palomino pony, with large grey spots, a grey mane, black hooves and eyes, and a red saddle and reigns.

It was beautiful, and much too grand to be stocked in any ordinary toy shop. Not that any toy shop would have contemplated stocking this particular horse, anyway. Like her dolls, and oversized children's clothes, Uncle Peter must have had it made specially for her. She knew that, not only because of its size, but also because she could see the knob of a shiny wooden dildo peeping up at her through a hole at the front of the saddle.

Uncle Peter placed her down on the saddle. It was made of real leather which felt cool and soft between her thighs. It felt comfortable. This was almost a perfect position for a woman to make love in, she thought. It gave her something to grip hard between her legs and gave her an amazing feeling of control.

She moved forward until her vagina was over the top of the dildo. Just beyond the hole there was a flap of wood

116

which was obviously there to stimulate her clitoris. She moved forward and pressed against it. The surface was rough, like a meat tenderiser, and gave a very satisfying touch. Uncle Peter handed Oscar to her and pushed her forward against the springs a couple of times. She gasped as her clitoris immediately reacted as intended. He bent over her and turned a knob bringing the dildo further up out of its hole. She shuffled back as she felt it pressing against her between her anus and her vagina.

He continued to rock her and adjust the length of the dildo ignoring her protests that she didn't want it any longer. At last he was satisfied and he went off to sit on the end of the bed to watch her. She rocked gently back and forth, feeling the long length of hard wood inside her. It was wickedly enjoyable and she felt the familiar stirring, but she needed more; just as he had known she would. To reach the flap of wood in front of the dildo and feel its coarseness pressing against the sensitive skin of her clitoris, she would have to take the full length of the wooden dildo inside her vagina.

And very soon she was doing just that.

She looked across at Uncle Peter. He looked back at her impassively, his face fixed with his permanent contended little smile. But he was pleased with her. She was sure of that. Her eyes began to loose focus and she turned away. She had no worries; she could concentrate on riding her wooden steed.

She closed her eyes and thought about her own part in Uncle Peter's fantasy. She saw a little golden haired girl, with an innocent face and big baby-blue eyes, sitting astride a fine wooden rocking horse. She held a cuddly teddy bear under one arm, and as she rocked backwards and forwards, a large wooden dildo constantly appeared and disappeared beneath the hem of her short white party frock.

Was it wrong, what she was doing? She still didn't know. But it was no use pretending that she was only doing it to fuel his fantasy. She found it incredibly erotic to know that he was sitting there watching her use his elaborate present to masturbate with.

After she had come, she left the dildo inside. Her muscles contracted round it as if trying to squeeze the last drops of non existent sperm from it. Then she relaxed the pressure of her legs and let the smooth hinged action of the horse move her back. She slid along its long polished length for the last time, and instead of stopping when she reached the knob, she let it slip free. Uncle Peter came and lifted her down from the saddle and took her into the bathroom, where he bathed her and dried her and put her into yet another new dress.

Susan had tea in the kitchen with Uncle Peter and afterwards they returned to her dungeon. They walked hand in hand over to the rocking chair, and still holding her hand, Uncle Peter sat down.

"Slip your dress off, sweetheart."

Susan did as she was told and he sat looking at her for several minutes. She didn't mind. It made her glow all over to know that he enjoyed looking at her like that.

"Turn round." His voice sounded hoarse with emotion.

She shuddered as his hands touched her hips and guided her back so that she was standing between his open legs. Then she jumped again as she felt the cold touch of the cream on her anus.

"Oh no, Uncle Peter, not that! Please! You're too big for me."

But it was too late. Uncle Peter guided her down towards his lap. She fought against him and as she did so his thumbs cut into her arms just above her elbows. He was supporting her weight, but also preventing her from moving away from him. His hands hurt; numbing her arms and bringing the tears to her eyes. And slowly they dragged her down, until she could feel his knob against the entrance to her anus.

It was no good closing her eyes and mind to it. That huge knob was laying siege to her private place and there was nothing to stop it. She felt it forcing the cheeks of her bum apart. In a moment, as her strength failed, it would force its way inside her, where it had no right to go. And then she would no longer be a child any more, she would be an experienced woman who had taken a man inside her secret place. The panic consumed her. She fought him with every ounce of strength in her body. But she was just a little girl, and he was a huge giant of a man, and the outcome was inevitable.

The cold cream had melted and become a warm liquid trickling down the crack of her bottom. It was uncomfortable standing with her knees bent and his thumbs cutting into her flesh. She knew that this was wrong and that it shouldn't be allowed to happen. But what could she do against him? She was a tiny little girl; small, alone, and insignificant, in a world which didn't seem to care. She felt him pressing hard against her entrance and she wanted to cry out in frustration. She felt the mouth of her anus expanding like that of a snake attempting to swallow an egg many times its size. She couldn't stop it. The thin cream covered lips rolled back upon themselves and continued to expand as they slid across the shiny surface of his knob. She gasped with pain as she waited to feel her flesh tear.

She started to scream.

Please God, he couldn't possibly be much bigger. No one could stand this pain. Soon they must reach the point of no return, from where it would be easier to go on than to go back. And then her straining lips would glide over the curved edge of his glans and precipitate her into a black abyss of martyrdom.

Suddenly he was inside her. She gave one last plaintive scream at the inevitability of it all. It was full of frustration, fear of the unknown, and despair at her loss of innocence. It was almost impossible to believe. How it had happened she didn't know, but that massive knob was now inside her. She was scared to move. She could feel it splitting her apart. It was so tight that it made him feel closer than anyone had ever been before. She could feel his warmth and the constant pulsating beat of his heart throbbing from within her own body. It was as if she was part of him, or as if he had taken over her body. This mustn't happen. He must know that he was too big.

She couldn't possibly accommodate it. She crossed her arms and dug her sharp nails into the back of his hands. That was a mistake, he released her arms and she slowly descended on him, a fraction at a time as her legs refused to support her own weight. She pleaded with him to help her, but she knew it was useless. And after a while, she became confused. Why was she protesting? Because she expected him to stop, or because it made it more exciting?

After an eternity of pain, she at last felt the rough material of his trousers against her bottom. And a moment later her full weight was bearing down on his lap. She had never felt like this before. She was completely full with a huge lump of living flesh throbbing and jumping inside her body. Was it possible? Where had it all gone? She didn't want to come. She hardly dared to move. But as soon as she allowed herself to relax and think about it, she shuddered to an immediate climax. She shook and groaned, and deep inside she felt the sudden discharge of liquid. Then her muscles were moving, rippling up and down the length of this strange foreign body which was forcing them apart.

His penis jumped and jerked deep inside her. Far deeper than she had ever expected anyone or anything to penetrate. She couldn't stand it. She had to move. But Uncle Peter held her tight, pulling her hard into his lap and preventing her from rising. She had to have relief and she started to wriggle and writhe against him. His weapon seemed to swell, then slip even further inside causing her to gasp. It must have trapped a nerve because she was paralysed, unable to even wiggle her bottom now. The paralysis moved out in every direction; creeping up her spine and down her legs until finally she couldn't move her toes, or tongue, or eyes.

"You must learn to sit still for your uncle, Susie. Just now and again when he wants a little peace. There will be plenty of time for you to play, afterwards."

His voice sounded strained. She sat perfectly still, staring into space, unable to speak or move, or even to blink. His hands moved to cover her breasts. He turned his face and rested his cheek against the back of her head. Then he started to play with her nipples. She felt them being squeezed between his fingers and thumbs. They felt hard and long, but it was as if they belonged to someone else. One part of her confused mind knew that they were her nipples and that she was entitled to the wonderful warm sensations which were emanating from them: but another part told her that she was stealing love which was meant for someone else.

She was at the centre of a strange white mist, and when he spoke to her it was with a disembodied voice which echoed in her head. It sounded as if it was coming from a vast distance away, from within a stone cavern hidden inside a mountain.

"Just relax and sit still, sweetheart."

She started to drift. She felt disembodied. Her legs were no longer part of her, nor anything above her breasts. But she must still have a body because she was aware of the massive member which was inside her. She could feel it holding her as firmly as if she was impaled on a stake. The pain made her lips tremble and filled her brain with a clamouring urgency which made it impossible to think of anything else. If only she could forget about the pain it would be quite pleasant sitting here in the middle of this white swirling mist where time stood still. But as it was, he was just too big for her.

His penis expanded and contracted inside her again and like a brain-washed dog she responded by discharging once more. There was nothing she could do about it. He had more control over her body now than she had herself. She was very wet; everywhere. The juices had dribbled out of her vagina and coated her inner thighs with their warm stickiness. And his penis was floating in another sea of juice. But the cushion of liquid hadn't deadened the pain. The sensations were still very intense and she could feel him very clearly and grip him very hard. It should have been wonderful, but it was just too much. She felt drained and ill. Again he flexed inside her, and again, like an obedient dog, she performed for him. She didn't know if she came in her vagina or in her anus. She just came. And kept coming on demand.

She pleaded with him to stop, but she wasn't sure if he could understand her, or even hear her. Her lips were thick and rubbery and seemed to move in all the wrong directions as she tried to concentrate on forming the words. Even her thoughts seemed slurred and she felt sure she must be jabbering incoherently. But when she shouted, he did stop. Sometimes he stopped for what seemed like several minutes. But then she felt the excitement rising inside her again. And although she did her best not to react to him, when he started to expand and contract his penis again, she was unable to stop herself reacting to him in the way that he wanted.

His hands were on her breasts and his lips on her neck. And the chair rocked gently back and forth, back and forth, back and forth. Slowly the dense white fog started to thin and become patchy allowing her glimpses of familiar features of her prison through its swirling mist. She heard the monotonous movement of the curved runners of the rocking chair as they moved back and forth on the padded floor. And she heard the sound of the regular creaking from its tired old joints. She fancied that she could even hear the quiet ticking of the alarm clock on the bedside table.

And now she was able to move again. The polished wood of the cross rail was beneath the balls of her bare feet. It was warm, friendly, and reassuring. She pushed against it raising herself up on the massive intruder who she held lodged deep within her chest.

The impossible had happened. She had stretched to accommodate him. Her passage was full of juice, but she was still so tight and he so big, that she felt every magnificent inch of him as she moved up his shaft. Uncle Peter helped her rise and it appeared to her as if his heavy knob bounced over every one of her ribs as it retreated out of her. He was even longer than she had imagined and she was forced to let herself sink back down on him long before his knob reached her entrance. But it was wonderful. The pain was fading now leaving a sensation of blissful wellbeing and endless love. She was enjoying the most incredible orgasm it was possible for anyone to experience.

This magnificent man was controlling his own desires and holding himself in check allowing her to use him to satisfy her own cravings over and over again.

At last she was satiated, but she didn't want him to leave her. She turned on his lap; careful not to release him. She laid her head on his chest and draped his arm over her, tucking his hand under her breast and closing his fingers around it so that her nipple was cupped in his palm. She pulled her knees up until one foot was on his knee and the other only a little below it. Then she wriggled her way down his shaft until she was comfortably full.

"I want to sleep now, Uncle."

She knew that she was being unfair. He had made her come and come until she was almost ill with exhaustion. He had held her tight and taught her how to accommodate his monstrous shaft. Then he had allowed her to use it to give herself total satisfaction. He deserved his reward. She should have made him come and then let him take his cock back and put it safely away inside his trousers. But she didn't want him to. Now that she knew how comforting it felt, hard up inside her, she couldn't bear to be without it.

"Alright, my lamb, you close your eyes and I'll rock you off to sleep."

She placed her thumb in her mouth and was asleep in a instant, aware that she was wrapped in love and safe in her uncle's protective arms.

They sat there like that gently rocking backwards and forwards as the evening slowly turned to dusk. Susan's eyes were closed, and she was drifting either side of sleep. But she could feel his gentle kisses in her hair and on the nape of her neck. She was home now; safe and happy and loved. She had no uncertainty about Uncle Peter's love, now. He wanted to use her, but there was no doubt that he loved her and that he would always protect her and make sure that no harm came to her. It was so comforting suspended in this post orgasmic dream. She let her mind drift again and dreamt of living in a world where her Uncle Peter held her tight and safe while she slept. And the pulse of his beautiful weapon kept pace with the steady beating of her own heart, but every so often it jumped and fidgeted inside her, to remind her that they were two separate people joined together in love.

He seemed perfectly content to indulge her wishes and allow her to sleep with his wonderful monster buried inside her. And for her part, she couldn't think of a more desirable way to remain. She wanted it to last for ever. Although, for the moment, she was fully satisfied and required no more sex, this was better than sex. It was the most wonderful cuddle she had ever experienced. She had everything. She had his love and kisses and comforting arms. And she still had his full attention. He was still hard for her and she was still wet for him. She could feel the juices whenever she wiggled her bottom like that. She smiled to herself as she felt him jump inside her and heard his sharp intake of breath as her movement brought him close to climax.

Would his cock be all wrinkled like a prune when she finally let him take it out? Poor Uncle Peter. Never mind, she would make it up to him once she had enjoyed a little nap. When she awoke, after sleeping with this ramrod inside her, she would want him then, like never before. And she would make him come like he had never come before. She wiggled her bottom again to reassure herself that she had the power, and almost giggled at his response. She had nothing to worry about there. She would blow the top of his head off. And she would call him Uncle Peter as he pumped into her like an erupting geyser.

CHAPTER 11

Suddenly the dungeon was bathed in bright light and she heard the commotion of several people descending the stone stairs. She jumped, opening her eyes and blinking in the unaccustomed brightness. She struggled to move, but Uncle Peter held her tight, soothing her and reassuring her that all was well. She was still curled up on his lap and unsure if she had dozed for minutes or hours. Her back was to the stairs and she was curious to know what was happening, but unable to see anything until Uncle Peter used his feet to turn the chair so that they could both see.

Three people were descending the steps, and although they weren't travelling fast, they were already almost at the bottom. In the lead was the Asian girl. She was nude and her arms were tied together behind her back with each wrist attached to the opposite elbow. Her long black hair was neatly tied up on top of her head and she wore a leather collar round her neck and was held on a lead by the blonde woman. The blonde was also nude, but instead of looking cowed and humbled like the Asian girl, she looked proud and triumphant, and she carried a short leather whip which she held like a badge of office. The third member of the party was Susan's master. He was fully dressed and looked relaxed and confident.

They paused as they reached Uncle Peter and herself and her master nodded at Uncle Peter and smiled. The blonde's green predatory eyes looked Susan up and down and her lip twisted in a contemptuous grin which made

Susan shudder with fear and press herself tightly against Uncle Peter's reassuringly huge frame.

Oscar had sat on his high seat, quietly watching while Uncle Peter and herself had made love. But as the blonde moved past him she struck him across the face with a hard downward swipe of her whip, toppling him to the floor. Susan jumped, shocked by the unexpected cruelty of her action. Uncle Peter laid his hand on her face pressing her head back against his chest protectively. The blonde pressed her whip into the Asian girl's back at the base of her spine and pulled back on the lead, forcing the girl forward in a stumbling motion which made her walk with her pert little breasts raised.

Uncle Peter put one arm under Susan's legs and the other behind her back and stood up. Susan looked down at Oscar. He remained where he had fallen, lying on his back, staring at the ceiling. He had suffered a loss of dignity, but he would feel better after a cuddle. Uncle Peter lifted her in his arms and, as he did so, she slipped smoothly from his still erect member. Suddenly she felt empty and abandoned. She squealed softly with surprise and disappointment and looked up at him in consternation. He smiled fondly back at her as she lay cradled in his arms, then lifted her towards his lowered head and kissed her eyes and then her lips. All was still well between them; she could relax.

"Come on, we'll go outside for a little sweet night air."

"Please," Susan pleaded asking him to return his lips to hers, and when he did so, she kissed him passionately trying to show him how much she loved his gentle protective kindness.

It was wonderful in the garden. Uncle Peter moved effortlessly with her in his arms as if her almost eight stone was nothing to him. The moon kept disappearing behind clouds, but he didn't seem to need it, appearing sure of where they

127

were going and not stumbling once. The garden was magical, full of heavenly smells, such as night-scented stock and honeysuckle. The only thing which spoilt it was her knowledge that Uncle Peter hadn't come yet. It still felt as if his wonderful weapon was still inside her and she wanted him to lay her on the soft dew-dampened grass and make love to her so that she could make him come. Instead, he carried her up a flight of wooden steps and started to lift her down.

"What is it, Uncle?"

He held her until she was sure of her feet then patted her on the bottom.

"You're going for a ride."

"Where?"

"High into the sky, right up where you can touch the stars."

One of the windmill's wooden sails was parked next to the steps and she instantly realised what he meant.

"No! I can't, Uncle. Please no, I'm scared of heights."

He took her by the waist and turned her upside-down. "You'll be alright, little one. Do you think your old Uncle would hurt you? It's lovely. And perfectly safe, you'll see."

She started to struggle, but he lifted her up by the ankles, holding both of them in his one huge hand. She squealed, but didn't dare wriggle any longer in case he dropped her. He fixed her right ankle to the wooden sail using a strap which was there for the purpose. Then he opened her legs and fixed her left ankle in the same way.

Susan continued to protest, but he ignored her terrified pleading and in a moment her wrists were also fixed and she was leaning back against the sail with its wooden slats pressed tight against her bottom and shoulders. He pulled a lever. She expected the sail to move immediately, but nothing happened. His hands returned to her right leg, running down both sides, from her ankle to her groin. His left hand lingered on her vulva for a moment before leaving to join his other hand on her left ankle. She hardly noticed. She was too tense with waiting for something to happen.

"Please, Uncle Peter, you don't understand, I'm terrified of heights."

Before he could answer, the sail gave a sickening lurch and her terrifying journey was under way.

The sail climbed slowly up, seemed to hang stationary at the top, and then raced down towards the floor again. Or was that just her memory of the Big Dipper? She was fairly sure that she made two complete revolutions before she dared open her eyes and start thinking again. The sails were set at an angle so that she felt as if she was lying on her back with gravitational force pressing her firmly against its slats. It felt reasonably safe, and quite comfortable. She started to relax and wonder if she was scared of heights after all. Perhaps she was really only scared of Big Dippers and open-rail stairs? The motion wasn't completely smooth, it jumped and vibrated at certain points, sending curious tremors through her body: and her heart into her mouth, as she feared the worst. But she even became used to that. The wood creaked and groaned continuously, as if protesting that it was old and should be left in peace. But the mill seemed huge and solid, and strangely reassuring. It was like being held in the grip of a huge giant which scythed effortlessly through the air with only the whisper of the passing wind as protest.

Her entire body was trembling now, with excitement for the danger, but also something else. As she reached the top of the revolution she pulled her eyes from the cloudy starless sky and looked out across the English Channel towards France a little more than twenty miles away. She could see the moonlight shining on the waves miles out to sea and count the navigation lights of at least ten vessels. Closer in, she could see a thin ribbon of road with tiny cars like Dinky toys on it. As she started to descend towards the black earth, she saw the brightly lit skylights of her own dungeon and through them the broken picture of the scene which was being enacted in there.

The Asian girl was tied to a spit over a fierce fire which lit her body with every shade of orange and red. Her master, bare to the waist, was slowly turning the handle of the spit. And the blonde was using a long carriage whip which curled itself round the other woman's defenceless body making her scream out in pain and terror. It was the most terrifying sight Susan had ever seen, and as she rushed towards the black earth, below the level of the dark surrounding trees, she felt a cold hand clutching at her heart and fancied that she could smell singing flesh amongst the wood and coal cinders.

The nightmare ride continued with Uncle Peter whooshing past in an upside down blur, and as she started to rise once more, she could see the moon coming out from behind a cloud and realised that it would be in time to fully illuminate her at the top of her revolution. She wondered at the people in the cars down on the road. Would they believe what their eyes told them? Would they be able to make her out with her white skin dark against the brighter whiteness of the painted sails? At last she was at the top of the revolution and fully lit by the eerie white light of the moon.

The sensation in her body was incredible. She hung there spread-eagled and nude, on display to anyone who cared to look at her, and it was wonderful. She wanted everyone in the world to look at her and admire her body. She wanted every man in the world to achieve an erection and long to make love to her. She felt very special. She looked at the cars on the road and was disappointed that they didn't suddenly swerve and crash as their drivers caught sight of the beautiful nude bound to the sail of the windmill. They continued on their way as if nothing had happened, but in her own mind she was convinced that everyone in the world would find her desirable.

Then she was descending again towards the horror in the dungeon. And she knew that she longed to hear the Asian girl's screams and see the whip cut into her flesh and the flames scorch that beautiful olive skin.

Susan lost count of the times she went round on the windmill's sail, but at last she felt the sails start to slow and realised that her trip was over. She felt cheated. She wanted to remain up there, sailing silently through the night sky, forty feet above the ground, completely nude and obscenely displayed to the whole world. She wanted to be left alone, with only the stars, the wind, and her own thoughts for company, as she ascended towards heaven's light at the top of the arc. Then she wanted to experience again the feeling of descending down into hell with the entire world suddenly filled with the horrific sight and sound of the poor tortured little Asian girl.

When Uncle Peter released her and turned her upright, she clung to him more desperately than she had ever clung to anything before. She wanted him now as she had never wanted a man before. She needed to feel him inside her without delay while every part of her body continued to tremble. But her brain and mouth wouldn't seem to work. She desperately wanted to tell him of her need, but she couldn't find the means to do so, and she fought him, trying to break free from his grip so that she could find his zip and release his member. And all the time, as she wriggled in his arms, her lips struggled against his and her teeth bit at him and her tongue thrust itself deep into his mouth.

They were back in the dungeon and she didn't know how. Her master was in front of her holding her hands. He crossed them and pulled her over a table. He held her in a firm grip so that her vulva was pressed hard against the wooden edge of the table and her bottom was raised in the air. Someone placed straps round her ankles, and pulled her legs apart, securing them to the legs of the table. She looked up in time to see the blonde wielding the whip. It curled round her bottom and she felt a white hot pain and heard the crack of the displaced air. It was quickly followed by the mortified cry of the terrified victim. Her brain tried to deny the truth, but that victim was her. She had been duped by her master and Uncle Peter and delivered into the hands of this female brute. The whip cracked again and again. Each time the white hot heat cut across her body and she tried not to scream or cry. And each time she failed.

She had become trained to the whip over the past two weeks, but this was different. This time she was being beaten by another woman. She looked up into the cold dispassionate eyes of her master, then over to the deep dark sympathetic eyes of the Asian girl. She noticed something else in those eyes; relief that it was someone else who was receiving this latest beating and not herself.

The Asian girl was still hanging upside down on the spit with her head hanging down so that she could watch what was happening to this latest victim. Susan looked at the honey coloured skin reflecting the glow of the flickering flames. It was criss-crossed with wicked looking slashes from her beating and Susan found it incredibly erotic.

Suddenly she was on fire. Her bottom twitched uncontrollably, begging for the cruel bite of the whip. Now she was lost; consumed with lust and ready to give herself to anyone who would take her. It no longer mattered that it was a woman who had induced this state in her programmed body. She had reacted as they knew she would. As she always must from now on. She looked at the blonde, pleading with her to strike her even harder, to punish her body and raise her orgasm still further. But the blonde smiled in triumph and stood back, curling her whip back against itself and holding it still in her hand in a gesture which signified that she had finished. Susan didn't understand. How could she be so cruel when she so desperately needed her to beat her harder than she had beaten a wretched soul before? Susan turned her eyes to her master to appeal to him, but he too was laughing at her need. And then she felt Uncle Peter's hands on her waist and knew that her salvation was in sight.

He entered her, penetrating her with such force that he drove all the breath from her body. She couldn't believe it. The ecstasy was more than anyone could stand. Far above the point where it could be enjoyable. She gasped in a mouthful of warm smoky air. It seared her lungs and was expelled almost immediately in an agonised scream as his massive rod shuddered to a halt inside her sending vibrations out to every part of her body.

It wasn't possible. No one could stand this level of emotion. She must faint. But she didn't and still he drove into her with each stroke harder than the last. And then at long merciful last he was coming. She raced to come with him. All thought of pain and injury were forgotten now. She could forgive him anything now. Bless him, he was coming at long merciful last. This was the second most wonderful man in the world. She would be good for him and fuck him as he had never been fucked before.

She thrust with him, matching him stroke for stroke. And when he stopped, as if suddenly struck by an assassin's bullet, she tightened her buttocks and gripped hard to his shaft. He remained perfectly still with his massive lance forced up inside her, unable to move. And she squeezed him tight and screwed every last ounce of sperm, energy, and love from him. She wanted all of him, to keep for herself, and to show him how much she loved and adored him. When she felt him fall on to her back, exhausted and totally empty, she smiled to herself contentedly.

She didn't mind at all about the massive weight which was almost crushing her spine. Her job was done. And well done at that. This massive giant of a man had been laid low by the love of a slip of a girl barely half his size. He might glory in being big, but being small had its uses as well. Her master released his grip of her arms. She looked up into his smiling eyes and knew that he agreed. She had done her work well and he was proud of her.

CHAPTER 12

Susan worked happily at her chores the next morning. It was a large house and there was a lot to wash, clean, and polish. But she didn't mind. He was a very exacting master who expected everything to be perfect. But no more exacting than she was herself. She took a pride in her work. In her mind, it proved her love for him. And, despite her aches and pains and the soreness of her body, as the jobs got done and everywhere began to look tidy and shine with cleanliness, she began to hum to herself.

Her work finished, she washed and prepared her body. Then she put on a white dress which had a short pleated skirt, white ankle socks, and white trainers. No bra or knickers of course. She still felt naughty and undressed without her knickers. It was nice. She watched herself in the mirror as she ran her fingers over her smooth vulva. It felt hot and slightly swollen, and it ached with anticipation. That was nothing new. It felt like that almost all of the time now. It was part of living in this wonderful house where anything might happen.

Reluctantly, she let her short skirt fall back over her nakedness, then smacked her right wrist with her left hand. Naughty. She must learn to be patient. She went to the kitchen and waited for both fingers of the large old pendulum railway clock to make their achingly slow accent to the twelve.

Exactly at noon, she tapped on his study door. Even though she did the same thing every day, she still felt the same excitement and fear when the rich chocolate brown voice she loved so much command her to enter. She made her way over to his desk and waited patiently for him to look up from a letter he was reading.

"Ah, there you are, Susan. How are you feeling today?"

"Very well, thank you, Master."

He took the letter and flicked it disdainfully into the pending tray. His dark brown eyes found hers. They looked harsh, almost angry, which made her stand even more stiffly to attention. Had she done anything wrong? Her terrified mind went flitting over recent events, investigating every possibility, however unlikely.

"You and I entered into an agreement when we first met."

"Yes, Master."

"You wrote pleading with me to let you be my slave, and I agreed."

"Yes, Master." Susan was almost in a state of panic now. Why was he reminding her of what they both knew? What had she done to displease him? Why was he talking to her this way? Please, whatever it was, please, God, let him punish me, but, please, please, don't let him send me away.

"You are a very beautiful girl, Susan. A very desirable girl. Any man would think so."

"Thank you, Master."

"And rich?"

"Not exactly rich, Master. more comfortable."

He didn't say anything and appeared to be waiting for her to elaborate.

"I have the house, and my parents' savings, plus the insurance money from the accident. It's more than I need, Master." Did he need money?

"And it gave you freedom."

"Sorry, Master?"

"It gave you the freedom of choice, to do what you wanted. To do anything you pleased. Or to do nothing, if that was what you wanted?"

"Yes, I suppose so, Master."

"And yet you chose to give all that up and become my slave?"

"Yes, Master."

"And now you have no freedom of choice at all. You do as you're ordered. Rise early and work like a dog. And expect nothing in return, other than the occasional kind word and a pat on the head. And more often than not you don't even get that. You get beaten like a dog instead, whenever the mood takes me."

"It's not like that, Master. You're a kind master. The work isn't hard, and I'm happy to be beaten. What pleases you, pleases me, Master."

"Really? Why's that?"

"It's what I want, Master."

"But why?"

"I want to serve you, Master. To obey every command you give me. To be the best, most obedient slave in the world. I only want to please you and make you happy. Nothing more." At last he had given her the chance she had been waiting for. The chance to declare her undying loyalty and love. But was it enough to save her? She longed to be able to tell him more. To be able to express herself better. To make him understand how much she needed him.

He suddenly stood up and turned his back to her. He stood there contemplating the books on the shelves. It was probably only for a moment, but to her it seemed like several minutes. She wondered if he had forgotten about her. Great men often have their mind's full of other things, and she had no doubt that he was a great man. His fingers walked over the spines of several books, caressing them like cherished old friends, but after a moment, he turned away from the shelves without selecting one. When he turned, she could see that he was still deep in thought and he walked past her without even noticing her. She remained at attention staring at the now empty chair behind the desk. And soon his voice came from behind her back."You want nothing more?"

"No, Master - except -" Her voice trailed away as she realised that she didn't have sufficient courage to tell him what he surely must already know.

"Except?" His voice was insistent.

"You, Master," she screwed her eyes closed, frightened of incurring his anger.

"Explain yourself."

"I'm sorry, Master."

"Don't be sorry. I'm not angry with you. Just tell me what you meant."

"I don't want anything else, Master. I have everything I want serving you. If you will allow me to do that it's all I need."

"Except? You said except."

There was no escape, she must tell him now. "I sometimes dream that one day you will make love to me, Master." She said this in a little voice. So little that she was worried that he might not be able to hear, and would be angry.

He didn't say anything. The time passed and she knew that he must still be there, but still he didn't say anything. She wanted to cry. She wanted to faint, or run from the room. She desperately wanted to turn round so that she could see what he was thinking. But she didn't dare do any of those things.

"You know that I'm a sadist?"

"Yes, Master."

"You know what that means? That I get pleasure from hurting you. By inflicting pain and humiliating you."

"Yes, Master." Just hearing him talk like that made her feel wet between the legs. She pushed her thighs together and bent her knees, hoping he wouldn't notice that she was no longer standing at attention.

"But of course, you knew that before you wrote to me."

"Yes, Master."

"Nevertheless, some of the things you've witnessed since you've been here - they must have shocked you?"

"Yes, Master."

"And yet you said nothing. And you have done nothing. You haven't asked to be released from your contract. And you haven't tried to run away."

"No, Master."

"Why is that?"

"I love you, Master."

"Even though I behave the way I do? How can you?"

"I don't know, Master. I'm sorry. I just do." She began to cry.

He came over to her and handed her a folded handkerchief. "Don't cry. I'm not angry with you. On the contrary, I'm very pleased with you."

She took the handkerchief gratefully, and wiped her eyes and blew her nose. "Thank you, Master."

She tried to hand it back, but he shook his head. "No, keep it. You may need it again."

He saw the sudden fear in her eyes, and did a strange and kind thing. He took her in his arms and kissed her. She had never been kissed like that before. She didn't understand what he was doing to her. The whole of her body came alive. The whole of her life was lit up. It was as if she had been dead before. Or perhaps asleep, like Sleeping Beauty? She started to shake, and when he released her, she couldn't stand. He tried to let her go, and she did her best, but her legs wouldn't support her. He tried a couple of times, then laughed, it was as if she were made of rubber.

He picked her up. She felt light, as light as a feather. And he must have thought so to, because he carried her effortlessly over to the settee. He set her down, then sat down himself beside her. He was smiling at her, waiting for her to recover. But how could she? She had known she loved him. But she had had no idea that it could be like that. She had had no idea what a single kiss could do.

"How can you love me?"

How could he ask that? How could he doubt her? And how could he expect her to answer such a question? He was the most important thing in her life. The only thing in her life. She would love him whatever he did. She had no choice. Why couldn't he understand that? He saw her look of desperation and realised that he was asking her an impossible question again. He laughed. "Alright, how could you have known you would fall in love with me when you wrote to me? You didn't even know me then."

"I did, Master, from your book."

This time his laugh was full of delight. Then surprise and disbelief. He saw that she was upset because he was laughing at her naivety and he shook his head to show that he didn't mean to hurt her feelings.

"And you think that there's part of me in that book?"

"Yes, Master, I'm sure there is."

He shook his head in disbelief. "If only."

"I'm sorry, Master, I don't understand."

"It doesn't matter. So we're agreed then. People may have different ambitions. But freedom is the same for everyone. The right to choose to do what they want to do with their lives, not what other people say they must do?"

"Yes, I suppose so, Master."

"And for you, true freedom means the freedom to choose to be a slave and have no freedom of choice at all?"

"Yes, Master." He was making her confused, but he must be right; that was what she wanted.

"And if I would fuck you, then you would have it all. Everything you had ever wanted from life. Heaven on earth?"

Was he laughing at her? And why had he used that awful word; was he trying to shock her? She felt close to tears again, but she knew that she was right.

"It's all I want. Master. I don't know if it's right or wrong. And I don't care. I love you, and I don't care if you're a monster. I would like you to love me, but it doesn't matter if you can't. However you feel about me, and however you treat me, I will still love you. Even if you send me a million miles away and I never see you again, I'll still love you. Even if you say you hate me and never want to see me again, I'll still love you. You are all I want, Master. And all I ask is that you let me be your slave. And if you can; if you don't find me too repulsive; that sometime; you make love to me."

This time his laughter contained genuine happiness. It was a wonderful sound. The most wonderful sound in the world. She had made him happy. She didn't understand why or how. But it meant that he was pleased with her and everything was going to be alright. He put his hand on her head and messed up her hair.

"Don't worry, Susan, no one could ever find you repulsive. Your beautiful, and so is your heart. It's a pity when such a sweet thing as you has to love a person like me."

"No, Master, please don't say that."

"I envy you, you know. It's a strange world where the slave has more courage and freedom than anyone isn't it, aye?"

"Yes, Master." She wished then, with all her heart, that she could give him the freedom he wanted. But she had no idea what it would take to set him free. The freedom to write the books he wanted, without interference? She longed to be able to make him as happy as he made her. And she knew that he was wrong about the book. Whatever restric-

141

tions had been put on him, she knew that there was still a large part of him in that story. She had felt it and fallen in love with it.

"I think I'm a very lucky man to have a slave like you, Susan."

"Thank you, Master. But not as lucky as I am to have you as my master."

"Oh dear, I think we had better leave our mutual appreciation at that before we start to make each other throw up." He laughed. But slowly the warmth went from his eyes and she knew that he was looking inwards again. And once more she experienced the feeling of foreboding. She felt very close to him then, and more than ever she knew that something was wrong. "Come on, lets go into the kitchen, there's some people you need to be introduced to."

CHAPTER 13

After the cool of his study, the warm air of the kitchen was comforting and friendly, and full of the aromatic smell of coffee. When she had left it a few minutes earlier it had been empty. Now it was occupied by three people. They were obviously all friends who enjoyed each other's company. They were sitting in a small group round the top corner of the battered old refectory table. There was Uncle Peter, the blonde woman, and the Asian girl. And they all looked up as Susan and her master walked in. They greeted her master, then turned their expectant smiles towards her.

"Uncle Peter you know of course. Quite well, by name, and reputation, and, er - a number of other things. And this is Margaret." Her master turned towards the blonde woman.

Susan took the blonde's outstretched hand. And without any hesitation, Margaret pulled her forward for a hug and a kiss on each cheek. "Well done, you've been very brave."

"I second that," the Asian girl said.

"Thank you," Susan said to Margaret, then "Thank you," she said again, as she turned to greet the other girl.

"And this is Orchid, who's lovely name is still insufficient to do full justice to her beauty." This time it was the beaming Uncle Peter who affected the introduction.

"These two rogues have been absolutely beastly to you," Orchid said seriously as she placed her tiny hand inside Susan's. Susan started to shake her head in denial, but the other girl pulled her forward with a giggle. "You must have loved it," she said as she kissed her first on one cheek. "I know I should have done!" She kissed Susan on the other cheek and dissolved into laughter at the wantonness her words revealed.

Uncle Peter pulled them apart. Orchid's laughter was so infectious that they were all laughing now. It was impossible not to. "Don't ever get like this one, Susie, whatever you do. It's a wonder my arm doesn't drop off with spanking her." He patted Orchid on the bottom to show what he meant, and she gave a little squeal of pleasure.

"That's because you don't do it properly, Peter. You're not hard enough on them." Her master was smiling and seemed almost as amused as they were, but that didn't stop him from going over to the big old Welsh dresser and taking a cane from the centre drawer. "Right, line up." He moved into the empty space beyond the far end of the table and drew a line in the air with the cane to show where he wanted them.

Susan looked at the other two girls, and Margaret smiled reassuringly and winked at her secretly, so that the men wouldn't see. Then both girls took a hand each and led her down to where her master was waiting. The three girls lined up, and all bent over and touched their toes when he ordered them to. He went along the line and used the end of the cane to flick their skirts up over their waists. Now Susan could appreciate the advantage of having so many mirrors in the kitchen. They mainly advertised brands of beer and spirits which were available in Victorian times, and Susan had thought they were old fashioned and a pig to keep clean. But now she was glad they were there. By looking in the one closest to her, she could see the reflections of the three bottoms in the one across the room. It was a sight worth seeing. Neither of the other girls were wearing any knickers either, so it was three beautiful little bare bums which she could see sticking up in a row.

Susan felt herself shudder, and saw her own bottom twitch as the erotic image made her body come alive with excitement and anticipation. At her side, Orchid began to giggle. Susan looked at her in the mirror. She was so beautiful. That wonderful oval olive face was full of happiness and mirth. But even so, when Susan looked at the little white teeth and the wonderfully curved pink cupid-bow lips, she could only think of how lovely it would be to kiss that sweet mouth.

She heard Margaret laughing, and when she swivelled her gaze to her other side, the blonde's gorgeous green eyes were also full of wicked mirth. Susan felt the laughter rising in herself, and soon they were all three giggling, like three naughty school girls up for the cane.

Her master passed down the line beating each one in turn. He had to do it four times before they finally stopped giggling. Then he did it twice more for luck. Susan could hardly believe it, and it wasn't only her bottom which was covered with a warm glow. The other girls had treated her just as if she was one of them. And so had her master. She had joined in their conspiracy, and their minor rebellion against her master's authority, and received exactly the same punishment as they had. It was wonderful. She looked at the three bottoms, each now with its criss-cross of new red weals, and she felt proud. They were all beautiful, she knew that. And her own was just as pretty as the other two.

Her master went along and kissed each of them in turn, letting his soft lips and probing tongue caress their stinging nether cheeks. He started with Orchid, and Susan watched the other girl's face, and sighed deep inside when she saw her begin to shudder as she came. Then it was her turn. He knelt down and placed one hand on each leg, just above the knee. And as soon as he did so she started to tremble as she felt the flood gates begin to open. When his lips actually touched the taught singing flesh of her cheek, there was no stopping her. She began to buck and twist as if she was receiving an electric shock from a live cable. He laughed with surprise and delight and ran his hands up her legs and took firm hold of her hips. Then he laid his cheek against her bottom, pulled her tight against his face, and rode with her until she had finished jerking and vibrating.

He left her before she was fully finished. She could have wished that he might have stayed a few seconds longer, but she couldn't be selfish. He passed on to Margaret and affected the same magic there.

His work completed, he left them like that and rose and crossed to the table where he poured himself a coffee. He sat down and smiled at Uncle Peter, then turned to look at the girls again. Appreciating that he didn't want to talk, Uncle Peter took up his newspaper and began to read. It was all quiet, except for the steady ticking of the stately old railway clock and the occasional rustle of the newspaper as Uncle Peter turned a page.

Her master seemed perfectly happy to sip his coffee and stare at them. His far-away look reminded her of the way she sometimes sat in the garden and let her eyes rest contentedly on a flower bed which she had just weeded and tided. She would sit there feeling the heaviness and pain in her tired body, and remember back to how she had wrestled with some particularly stubborn weed before finally subduing it. Then she would imagine how neglected and untidy the bay had looked before all her hard work, and congratulate herself on how much better it looked now. There was a special kind of satisfaction in contemplating a job well done. It would need to be done again, of course, in the not too distant future. But meanwhile, it was a joy to behold.

Susan looked at the reflection of Margaret's vulva in the mirror. Her labia were swollen and made shiny by an abundance of lubricating juices. Her wetness had darkened the blond hair nearest to the glistening pink lips, while that

146

further away was still fair and perfectly dry. She realised that Margaret was watching her, so she cut short her inspection and raised her gaze to hers. The two women smiled contentedly at each other in the mirror. Margaret's eyes were dark and dreamy and a little glazed. They were like two limpid green pools hidden deep within a secret wood which shaded out all light. But they didn't fool Susan any more. Deep beneath the cool surface she could see the satisfied sparkle of happiness. The happiness of a woman who knows she's loved.

Susan turned to look at Orchid. It was the same story there. Her raven-black muff was sprinkled with powdered diamonds of love juice. And the huge hazel eyes were full of love and contentment. Her master had three very happy women in that cosy kitchen. No wonder they all wanted nothing more than to love and obey him.

Anywhere else it would have seemed strange, to think of the two men sitting sharing a cup of coffee like any two friends, while a row of obedient young girls stood clutching their ankles with their bare bottoms raised high into the air. And it should have seemed bizarre to witness the pride and pleasure the girls were deriving from being allowed to display the obvious signs of their recent chastisement. And it was true that Susan would never again be able to look at a tidily dug flower bed without remembering back to this moment. But somehow, none of it felt strange, or bizarre, or at all out of place. Not here. Not in the lovely old mill which had seen so much of human behaviour over the years. Here, it seemed perfectly right and proper. The mill had observed the generations come and go; each with their different worries and ambitions. And it wasn't unhappy about this latest generation. They were happy and full of love, living life the way it should be lived by everyone.

Her master looked at his watch. "Well, we can't have you three standing about doing nothing." He placed his coffee cup back in the saucer and stood up. "Not when there's the lunch to be served." He walked along the line using the cane to flick each short skirt back over each bare bottom. Then he walked back to the dresser and put the cane away. He clapped his hands. "Come on, jump to it, I'm hungry. How about you, Peter?"

"I'll say. Could eat a horse, Old Boy."

But no one was really listening. The spell was broken and the moment was past. The happy giggling girls raced about bumping into each other and getting under each other's feet as they rushed to make everything ready for a perfect family feast.

For Susan it was the best meal she had ever eaten. Everything tasted better than it had ever tasted before, just as if she was really tasting it for the first time. This was the happiest she had ever been. She could hardly believe it was actually happening to her. She kept looking into the many mirrors as if to reassure herself that she was actually there, part of this happy gathering. And there she was, happy and smiling, wild eyed and animated, flushed in the face, and excitedly sharing in their laughter and conversation. At that moment she could finally believe that she would have everything she had ever wanted. She was one of them. Accepted and respected for what she was by people who understood her needs and desires. Wonderfully exciting, beautiful people, who knew all about life and how to enjoy it. And she was to become one of them.

The girls especially were really excited about the displays which they had put on for her. She freely admitted that she had been fooled; that she had honestly believed that they were poor innocent little victims of the two cruel scheming men. Then, of course, they had wanted to know the truth. Wasn't she just a little bit disappointed now that she knew that it had all been a pretence to excite and test her? Wasn't she a bit disappointed to discover that she wasn't actually living in a house where the men were as genuinely wicked and devious as she had imagined? And she had been forced to own up, and admit that she was.

Her bottom was still singing from the heat of her recent beating. Her brain was singing from the strength of the wine, the talk and laughter, and the love and friendship. Uncle Peter's hand was on her inner thigh, absently stroking it and sending tingles of desire cascading out into every part of her body. And best of all, every now and then, she caught her master's eye. And when she did, her heart leapt, and for a split second she felt certain of him. Certain that she had seen desire for her in his eyes. But then, immediately afterwards, she was uncertain again. Worried that she might have been mistaken. Convinced that she wasn't worthy of him. Terrified that it might only be wishful thinking.

But, if only it could be true. If only he could want her. The thought was almost too much to bear. The thought of him touching her, kissing her, entering her. Her life would be complete. She would never ask for anything more, ever again. If she could just have him once; feel him driving into her, taking her completely; making her his. She would be content then, happy to remain loyal, obedient, and patient for ever more. Happy to scrub and clean for him; to cook and wash for him, and always, to make herself desirable and available for him. She would ask for nothing else. She would be happy to remain his willing slave, never asking for anything more, but always living in hope.

Then it was over, and Uncle Peter and the two girls left to pursue their own pleasures. And she was alone with her master again. Now she was sure. This was to be it. She had passed all his tests and they were all pleased with her. The girls liked her. Uncle Peter liked her. And her master liked her. She was sure of that. Most of the time, he still looked at her fondly, as a father would look at a daughter. But

149

there were those other times when he looked at her with desire.

"Come on, we'll go to the study." He smiled as he spoke and she felt the excitement racing through her body again.

She was still intoxicated with the wine and the party atmosphere, but now there was something else all together more overwhelming. This was it; she was about to get her reward and become part of his family of friends. She wouldn't let him down. She worshipped him, and it was sure to make her over responsive. But she wouldn't disappoint him. She would make it good for him. She would make him happy and show him how enjoyable she could be.

He walked round the desk and sat down. If desks were classified like war ships, then this would have been the biggest class of aircraft carrier. It was massive, and it divided them. It cut her off from him and made her feel small and frightened.

"You have done well so far, but there's more to come."

She heard his words, but couldn't accept them. They were like a slap in the face. He was continuing to speak, and she heard and understood what he was saying. But still, every ounce of her body rejected it and refused to believe it was true. It must be a dream, or another awful wicked joke.

Her knees bent and she knew she was going to faint. She put out her hands reaching for the edge of the desk; not to save herself, but to ward herself off so that her falling body wouldn't crash into it. She had let him down. She should have been able to remain at attention and listen to his terrible pronouncement on her future. But she couldn't. Her poor brain couldn't take any more.

She felt his hands on her body, holding her round the waist and under the arms. He leant her against his knee and without opening her eyes she realised what must have happened. He had come round the desk and caught her, now he was sitting on the desk letting her rest, half sitting, against his body.

She felt him run his hand through her hair. Felt her hair rise and then flick back into place. Then she felt his cool lips on her forehead. And once more felt him lift her and carry her to the settee. He sat her down, and she crawled into the corner; forcing herself against the thick padded arm and back. She curled herself up, returning to the womb. She pulled her feet up under her bottom and held them there. She was behaving very badly. He must be angry with her. But she couldn't help it. He should have warned her. He shouldn't have acted so kind. She could have taken it if he had been firm with her.

He took her fingers and wrapped them round a high-ball glass. The glass had come straight from the cold shelf in his own fridge. It was frosted with condensation and stuck to her skin. It contained ice and lemon, and a clear liquid. She lifted it to her lips and drank. It was only water. Lovely cold refreshing water. She held the glass to her forehead and smiled weakly. "I'm sorry, Master, I've let you down."

"Don't worry. You stay there and recover. When you're ready we'll go on." He turned and walked back to his seat behind the desk.

Didn't he care? Or was he being cruel to be kind? She sighed. She would have to cry, she knew that. But not now. Now he was waiting for her to show that she could be a good and obedient slave, and she mustn't let him down. Not again. Never again. She would be strong and ask nothing. Expect nothing. Accept everything, however cruel. And wait. But wait for what? What would be left if he sent her away? She sighed, and he looked up. She saw his movement from the corner of her eye and looked over at him. He should have been unobtainable, waiting coldly behind that massive desk. Waiting for her to recover enough for him to pass final sentence on her. But he wasn't. She saw the look in his eye and knew that she was sitting so that her naked bottom and vulva were exposed. Almost before she had time to think, her hand moved to her vulva and her fingers brushed lightly over it, from top to bottom, following the line of her slit. It was enough, she didn't want to make him angry. Only show him that she knew that he wanted her really. Their eyes remained locked for a moment longer, then she dropped her gaze and began to untangle her body and stand up.

Once more, when she stood at attention in front of his desk, he began to tell her his arrangements for her again.

"Tomorrow morning, at six o'clock, a man will call for you. A stranger. He will be your new master. You will go with him and do everything he says without question. You will treat him the way that he stipulates, but you will obey him exactly as you would me. Do you understand?"

"Yes, Master."

"You will not let me down. Your behaviour reflects on me. There must be no further lapses, understood?"

"Yes, Master."

"You'll give him this." He laid a small sued leather wallet on the desk. It was the size of an A5 sheet of paper and had her interwoven initials, SD, embroidered in the centre of the flap. She recognised the golden threads. They had been taken from the lock of hair she had enclosed with her letter pleading with him to let her become his slave. It made her vulva itch with the memory of when it was covered with the same golden locks.

She wanted to speak; to ask all manner of questions, but she didn't dare.

"It contains your contract. And a letter. It's official, all properly signed and sealed. As from six o'clock tomorrow morning he will be your master for ever more, unless he wants to dispose of you of course."

He looked at her. And this time, she didn't need a mirror to know how she looked. She was white. As white as chalk. She felt white, and weak, and drawn, and old. She only wanted this to end now. So that she could be alone with her misery. If she had been a different person, she might have hated him. But she couldn't hate, and especially not him. She loved him still, even though he had done this to her. In fact, because he had done this to her, she loved him even more. Fifteen minutes ago she had been happy. Possibly the happiest person in the world. Then he had seemed almost obtainable. Now she knew how ridiculous she had been to ever think so. He was more unobtainable, and desirable, than ever.

"I have included a letter, making my recommendations. But that's all they are now; recommendations. You know the terms of the contract. So you know that you are his to do with as he pleases." He held out the leather pouch and she took it. "I won't require you any more today. Go back to your room and spend the time as you please."

"Thank you, Master," is what her words said, but her body and eyes pleaded with him not to do this. Even now, she still hoped for a last minute reprieve.

"I won't ever see you again, so I will say goodbye. You have been a good slave to me, Susan. I hope your new master will be as pleased with you."

"Thank you, Master."

"Run along now, off you go."

"Yes, Master. Thank you, and goodbye."

"Goodbye, Susan." And that was it, he looked down at his papers and she was dismissed from his mind and life for ever.

CHAPTER 14

The next morning she stood in the hall waiting.

She looked at herself in the full length mirror. She was wearing what would probably be described as a pink denim suit. Although there didn't seem nearly enough of it to warrant such a grand description as suit. It consisted of a waistcoat and wrap-over skirt. The waistcoat left her arms and shoulders and a large proportion of each breast bare; she would need to be careful not to bend down in front of anybody.

The matching skirt was cut on similar lines. That is, by someone who seemed to be acutely aware of the high cost of raw materials these days. It was probably no more than 14" long. And it flared out from her body, especially over her bottom, which it hardly seemed to cover at all. She lifted the flap of the skirt up and took a peek. A tiny triangle of shiny pink satin and silk peeped back at her. It was a G-string, so at the back there was only a thin cord, most of which was lost to view between the cheeks of her bottom.

The outfit was completed by a shoulder bag, and a pair of open-toe mules. These were also both made from pink denim. The mules had very high wooden heels. Standing on them was like trying to balance on the side of a hill. She continually felt as if she was about to launch herself into space. But the bag was quite nice, big and shapeless and easily held all her worldly goods.

Besides her own gold watch her only jewellery was to be a large pair of gold bangle earrings. Again, they were not what she would have considered choosing for herself.

But now that she saw herself in them, she had to admit that they did something for her. They matched her short golden hair, and somehow just added the right finishing touch to her face. They also added the right finishing touch to her little pink outfit.

This wasn't the Susan Dixon who had been brought to this mill only a few weeks ago. That pale little mouse didn't exist any more. She had been replaced by this beautiful confident creature who had the courage to dress like this and stride out into the world unashamed. She looked at the contrast between the golden glow of her lightly tanned skin and the pastel pink denim. Her firm brown thighs, long shapely legs, smooth round shoulders, and perfectly curved breasts shone with all the health and energy of a top athlete in peak condition. But the delicate tone of the pastel pink cotton left no doubt why this particular body had been honed to perfection. She was all woman. But still very feminine, and not too much woman for a man.

The doorbell!

She snatched Oscar up from where he had been sitting on the old fashioned hat stand and she was the frightened little girl again, clutching her teddy to her chest for comfort.

She swung the big heavy door open and looked up at the man who stood patiently waiting on the other side.

The morning sun was behind him, blinding her and shading out his face. It struck the tight curls of his hair and surrounded his head with a golden halo. The beautifully soft brown hair also curled out from the 'V' of his canary-yellow polo shirt, and covered his deeply tanned arms and hands with a light down.

She knew that she ought to say something, but she couldn't. He moved forward a pace, and now his head blocked out the sun. He was tall; six-foot-two. Well built; fourteen stone. And handsome. With his sparkling blue eyes and long curly chestnut-brown hair, he was the closest thing Susan had ever seen to a Greek god. If the time ever came when women were allowed to design their own ideal partner there would be a lot of men who would look just like this.

"I'm Mario." The voice was soft and confident, with a laugh in it. And something else - a certain pride.

She remembered to close her mouth before trying to reply. He wasn't what she had expected, and he was standing very close, confusing her.

"S-s-susan."

"Do you have a lisp, Susan?"

"Y-y-yeth."

There it was then. She saw that old familiar look in his eyes and felt the heat rising up from her breasts to bathe her upper body and face in shaming pink. Why did it always have to be like this?

"Come."

She stepped out to join him on the top step and he swung the door shut behind her. It closed with a loud bang which she heard echoing down the hall into the bowls of the silent old house. It was finished. Her life there was done.

The tall trees that surrounded the mill prevented her from seeing the van until they were actually out in the lane. Then she stopped in her tracks, staring at it in amazement. It was huge and grey with a picture of a herd of stampeding wild horses on the side. The paint-work was beautiful. The picture looked like a scene from a film which had been projected on to it's side then imprisoned there beneath several inches of enamel and wax. She could even see her own reflection in it, standing there open mouthed clutching her teddy.

He stood on the step, and, reaching up, opened the passenger door and swung it wide.

She looked at him wide eyed, uncertain what to do. He placed one hand on her arm and the other on her bottom, and suddenly she was gliding effortlessly upwards through the air. She snatched hold of a long chrome handle and the next moment she was inside the cab, and a different world.

She had never seen inside a cab like this before and she had taken it for granted that it would be rough, with cheap plastic surfaces, no carpets, and uncomfortable seats smelling of oil. But this was the height of luxury. The seats were leather and big enough and thick enough to curl up in to drift off to sleep. The dashboard was also of leather and polished wood and fitted with enough instruments and gadgets to keep the most enthusiastic airline pilot happy.

The other door opened and he swung himself up and into the driver's seat. She stole another glance at him. The strong warm sensation of his hand on her bottom hadn't faded and she felt a strange excitement at belonging to this stranger, for belong to him she undoubtedly did.

"Here we go."

She had the impression of a boyish grin and a flash of perfect white teeth, then they were under way and the big shiny giant was lumbering down the lane. She was way up in the air. It was like viewing the world through a huge picture window from the upstairs room of a luxury apartment while enjoying all the fun of a fairground ride. The huge wheels climbed in and out of the giant pot holes making the body snake up and down like the human dragon at a Chinese festival. And Mario pulled on the air-horns, continually blasting out the same cheerful derogatory tune: 'Hitler, he's only got one ball!' Her memory dragged the words from some long forgotten recess. She thought of her master working away in his quiet study, and she started to smile. This din would be driving him to distraction.

She felt her new owner's hand on her inner thigh. She could feel the heat of it through the denim skirt. She stiff-

157

ened and sat bolt upright, struggling to come to terms with the shock. People didn't do that. At least, no one had ever done anything like that to her before. Then she felt the rush of electricity and guilt coursing through her body. It was as if he had caught her out in her disloyalty, not only to him, but to her true master. 'You will not let me down. Your behaviour reflects on me. There must be no further lapses,' that was what he had said.

She could feel the excitement and tension in the stranger's touch. It felt tentative and eager, and not at all like her true master's firm confident caress. She turned to him and smiled. Reassured, he turned back to look at the road. And as he did so, she let her gaze drop to his lap to confirm her suspicion. His slacks were pulled tight over a large bulge.

He swung the vehicle out on to the coast road and they were off at last, going God knew where. Once he had changed up the gears, he returned his hand to her leg. This time caressing up and down her naked flesh, from her knee to the start of her skirt.

She had no objection any more. She was his to do with as he liked. Her true master had done a good job after all. She took the leather pouch from her bag and handed it to him. "My contract. And a letter from my previous master, Ma-ma-." It wasn't a true stutter this time, she didn't know which to say, was he to be Mario, or Master?

He looked at her. The sparkling blue eyes were laughing at her, willing her to make the wrong choice.

"Master."

He nodded his satisfaction.

There, it was done. Her true master would never hear any bad reports about her. Not one.

"What does the letter say?"

"I don't know, Master. It's sealed with wax."

"So you looked then?"

He had caught her out, already. She shouldn't have opened the pouch and looked inside. It was for her new master, from her old master, and no concern of hers, a mere slave. She had let her true master down.

He looked at her face, and seeing her concern, seemed unable to stop himself. He threw back his head and laughed. His laugh was loud and deep and full of genuine enjoyment. It was a sound which was as fine and true as a peel of perfectly matched church bells. A sound which she was destined to hear many times in the future, and always with the same effect. She began to laugh herself. She tried to suppress it, but it was impossible.

He turned the wallet over in his hand, taking a cursory glance at both sides, then discarded it, tossing it contemptuously on to the dash board as if it had no worth at all. His hand returned to her leg, this time with far more confidence.

CHAPTER 15

They were quiet again for several miles. Then he said: "Important things first," and turned to her and smiled.

The regular tick-tocking of the indicator told her he was about to turn off, and a few minutes later they shuddered to a standstill outside a Happy Eater. She was a little disappointed that it wasn't a proper trucker's pull-in, but she was happy enough for the opportunity to stretch her legs.

He came round the cab and took her by the waist and lifted her down. Once inside she realised how absolutely ravenous she was and was happy to eat anywhere which served bacon, eggs, and hash browns. They ate their breakfasts and ordered more tea and toast. Now she was really into it. She giggled at her own wickedness as she looked at the menu trying to decide which fattening dessert would go best with a massive fry-up.

"Are you wearing any knickers?"

His question took her by surprise, and she looked at him over the top of the menu with a certain amount of curiosity, wondering what on earth had made him ask. "Yes." She would like to have added: 'of course,' but realised that that would be pushing things a bit too far these days.

"Give them to me."

"What! Here?" She looked round. It wasn't crowded, only a few businessmen: and two families, one noisy and one quiet.

He nodded. It was a familiar enough gesture which on this occasion took her breath away and sent the adrenaline rushing through her body like a headless chicken. She placed the menu down and looked round again. The staff and customers were all occupied with their own lives. Suddenly, with a cold certainty, she knew that she was going to do it. Her hair stood on end and she felt her nipples rub against the inside of her waistcoat. She lifted herself from the seat so that she was about an inch above it, then put her hands under her skirt and quickly pulled the G-string free of her waist and down onto her legs just above the hem of her skirt.

She was boiling hot now and her heart was in her throat. Mario was no use. He just smiled at her confusion as if he was highly amused by it all. For all his look told her, everyone in the place could be staring at her, too disgusted and amazed to say anything about her outrageous behaviour. She looked round, swivelling her head in every direction. She did her best to make it appear as if she was just taking a casual interest in her surroundings during a lull in their conversation. No one was looking at her. The staff were busy cooking and serving, and the customers were happily going about the business of taking breakfast in a Happy Eater, where, as everyone knows, nothing naughty or unusual ever happens.

She pushed her knickers over her knees and felt them slide down her smooth legs to her ankles. Another casual look round before bending over to take a tissue from her bag. It was all too easy, except that they caught on the stupid heel of her stupid shoe. But she didn't panic, not too much anyway. And once she stopped jerking at them hard enough to wrench them in two, they almost fell free of their own accord. When she sat up again they were safely hidden inside her closed left hand.

She took one last look round while dabbing the beads of sweat from her upper lip with the tissue. Then she was holding her hand out to him across the table, palm down, with her knickers hidden inside her closed fist.

He made no attempt to take them from her. He merely looked at her with that supercilious little smile on his face. Then he nodded to show that she should open her fist and let them drop onto the table. She looked at him in amazement, but did as he demanded. She withdrew her hands and sat with them clenched together in her lap. And she stared with fixed eyes at the little pink cobweb. It looked so innocent and insignificant, like a little dab of candyfloss on the cream Formica table top.

She didn't dare to turn round again. Now she was sure that everyone must be looking at the back of her head, and the bright red tips of her ears. She looked at him again and still didn't understand. What was he doing? There was no denying that it was erotic. While there remained the faintest possibility of being found out her body would continue to behave as if she was taking a white-knuckle ride in the nude through a theme-park crowded with happy laughing families.

Was that it? Were they playing chicken? Well if they were, he had won. She reached out her hand to retrieve the whisper of pink satin and lace, but his reactions were far quicker than hers. He placed his right hand on the table with his index finger through the loop of the waist band. Now, if she tried to snatch them back they would snag on his finger and force a public tug-of-war.

Even without turning round she was aware that their waitress was on her way with their extra order of toast and tea. She looked at Mario silently pleading with him to pick up the offending garment and put it safely out of sight under the table. But he ignored her, lifting his eyes to smile over her shoulder at the approaching waitress. Susan swayed to the left to allow the young woman to bring the tray in and place their tea and toast on the crowded table top.

"Thank you." Mario's eyes met those of the waitress who almost curtsied in her confusion as his beaming smile cracked his face apart and lit up her day.

"Thank you, Sir."

When she had gone he lifted the knickers to his nose and delicately sniffed them, all the time watching her reaction. Then he poked them into his top pocket. Their dark outline hardly showed through the pale cotton. And the flimsy construction hardly caused a crease to spoil the smooth lines of his crisp yellow polo shirt.

At that moment Susan's arm was barged aside by the bullet hard head of a four year old girl. The little angel had a rag doll firmly fixed under one arm and something else clutched in her other hand. Tiny knickers!

Before they could stop her, the little madam reached up on tip toe and placed them firmly down in the centre of the table. They both looked at her in amazement, horrified by the intense concentration in her wide sky-blue eyes, and the knowledge of the gift she had presented to Mario.

"Emma!" The woman's frantic scream made everyone jump and the pair of white knickers were snatched from the table almost before either of them had time to be certain what they were.

"I'm so dreadfully sorry. She's never done anything like this before. Never!" The woman lifted Emma up and rushed her from the restaurant.

Susan was left with a lasting impression of the girl peering over her mother's shoulder with those huge innocent blue eyes still beaming out her undying love for the horrified Mario.

CHAPTER 16

Susan became aware of how warm and comforting it was in Mario's arms, and of the closeness of his body. He smiled into her eyes as he undid the buttons of her waistcoat. She looked over his shoulder, but there was nothing to see. He had pulled the wagon up on to some waste ground and parked it a few feet from the high blank wall of a derelict building. They wouldn't be disturbed. And it was just as well. This man wasn't like her true master, she knew that. He wouldn't make her wait. His own desire would see to that. And she was still unsure how she felt about that fact.

He was beautiful, there was no denying that. Any woman would find him desirable. And yet. There was something. She couldn't put it into words, but there was something lacking. She was about to experience what it was like to make love to another man. She hadn't been with enough men to find that prospect anything but exciting. And not only was this man gorgeous, he was also almost a stranger. And finally, he was her new master with the virtual power of life or death over her. No wonder she was shaking from head to toe. And yet. There was still that doubt. Was this really the sort of man that her true master thought she wanted?

She looked into his eyes, trying to decipher the secrets which lay behind them. That was pretty easy at the moment. There was no doubt that he liked her boobs. He took so long looking, that for one horrible moment she wondered if she had been wrong about him. Perhaps he did only want to look and savour and make her wait until she felt she would burst.

But she needn't have worried. Finally, at long last, the beautifully calloused hand descended and the wait was all worth while. As it touched her naked breast she tried to suppress her sigh of gratitude. But it was no good. It forced its way out, sounding all jerky as she trembled under the gentle caress. He manoeuvred her nipple to the very centre of his palm, and holding it there, began to slowly rotate his hand. His touch was smooth and light, almost reverential, but it set up an ache in her groin which fed a little whisper of doubt in the back of her mind. Was she right about her true master, or was this to be the special one?

He bent and kissed her breasts like a Frenchman greeting two long lost friends. Her eyes closed and her heart beat faster. He pulled each nipple into his mouth one at a time, like a hungry little boy sucking spaghetti. He passed back and forth from one nipple to the other, holding each in turn in the 'O' of his lips and keeping it trapped there while he slid it up and down his probing tongue.

Then he forgot himself completely and turned wild. All pretence of restraint and finesse was abandoned as he squeezed her breasts together, and scrambled both nipples into his mouth at the same time. And once he had them safely in, he tried to swallow them, forcing them all the way to the back of his mouth where he started to chew at them with his back teeth. The pain was almost unbearable, but she didn't dare cry out too loudly in case he thought she wanted him to stop. And he mustn't do that. She never wanted him to stop. So she whimpered and sobbed and begged him for more.

Please let this be the one! He slipped her waistcoat off over her shoulders and her treacherous body conspired with his soft lips as they took possession of all her newly revealed flesh. He abandoned her nipples, leaving his fingers and thumbs to deal with them as his lips went off to travel down her stomach to her belly. There, his tongue forced its way into her navel and set up a direct link to the very back of her vagina. Then he was off again. This time travelling upwards, back to her breasts, but only lingering there for a moment, before wandering slowly over to her neck. She couldn't stand this. It was too much. He was driving her insane. She tried to put her head down to catch those elusive lips in her own, but he was too quick for her, and once more he was off. This time they travelled across her shoulder, and down her arm to the very tips of her fingers. Everywhere they had visited was left tingling with longing for their return, and everywhere they were yet to go was left panting with expectation.

Oh Master, I'm sorry! She arched her back to tighten her stomach as his hair brushed against her breasts tickling her and making her shudder with desire again. Once more, the tip of his tongue entered her navel, and his hand moved from her knee onto her inner thigh. Since his last visit, her navel had been given time to think about it, and this time, as his tongue burrowed its way inside, she felt the first release of juices deep within her vagina. Meanwhile, his hand continued to travel gently backwards and forwards along her upper leg. With each caress the movement increased until it was moving the full length of her inner thigh from her knee to her crutch. Then it stopped at the wrong end, and stroked her knee, going round and round and getting nowhere while her vulva was crying out for it. But somehow it must have heard that cry, for, ever so slowly, it began to make its determined way back up her leg.

It was so strange to feel this new touch on her body. His caress was slow and gentle. It was almost as if he was playing with her like a poacher tickling a salmon. And for her part, she felt like a virgin, waiting with bated breath for her lover's finger to finally reach her vagina for the first time.

She couldn't bear the tension any longer. She couldn't sit there passively waiting. Not any longer. And merely writhing and wriggling weren't enough any more. Something more drastic was called for. She reached down, and taking his head between her hands, lifted it up to where she could reach those tantalising lips. She clamped her mouth to his and pushed her tongue inside as far as it would go. He was very different, but was he the one? Not that it mattered too much any longer. Not at the moment. She needed him so desperately that for the next few minutes true love would have to take a poor second place to even truer lust.

She kissed him long and hard. And he responded, but part of him still hung back, reluctant to give her everything. She released her buckle and unwrapped her skirt. Then raised herself off the seat for long enough to pull it free. She kicked off her shoes and screwed up her toes. Somehow the discarded skirt had found its way under her feet, and, thankfully, she gripped it hard with her toes. Now she was as naked as God intended.

"You have no idea do you?" His voice was almost a whisper filled with awe.

"What?"

"How very beautiful you are. And how beatable!"

He reached up and pulled the rear-view mirror down until she could see her own face in it. She was flushed and her eyes were wild, but otherwise she looked the same as usual. She saw a girl with wide light blue eyes clearly picked out with black eye-liner and her golden layered hair all higgledy-piggledy. Her face was sweetly pretty with a little straight nose, pointed chin, and virtual cupid-bow lips. She looked clear eyed and excited like a fourteen-year-old all keyed up and ready for some mischief.

He moved the mirror on down her body. Her breasts were large, round, and firm, with the lightly tanned skin pulled tight and the small dark pink areolae crowned with large stiff nipples. The mirror moved on over her tight stomach, and stopped, leaving the top of her thighs and her bare vulva framed in the oblong of mirrored glass.

Her vulva was as bare as a baby's. But she wasn't a baby, and for some reason that made it seem obscene. Her bald mound should have been covered with tight golden curls; a dense magical jungle which she had delighted in making a hiding place for her little pink fingers since as long ago as she could remember.

He was staring at the image in the mirror as if he was spellbound. It was as if he was undergoing a religious experience and she didn't want to hurry him or spoil it for him, but her breasts were in desperate need and could wait no longer. She guided his head to them and pressed his face firmly against her right nipple.

"Bite them please, Master. Bite them! Bite them!"

He needed no further bidding and this time she made no attempt to suppress her groans of relief as he chewed at her nipples with ever increasing firmness. Now her inner labia were moving again. She could feel them unfurling and growing even fatter. Suddenly it was all too much. She screamed and threw her legs apart, thrusting them straight out in front of her, stretching them to their furthest limits. She beat at his head and pulled at his hair until he let go. She was sobbing now, partly with pain, partly with desire, but mainly with frustration.

She pulled his mouth on to her left breast, all the time still whimpering with desire. She couldn't speak. She didn't want to speak. He must know what she wanted without her telling him. He must understand that there was a direct route between her nipple and her vagina which only pain could open up for her. And he did understand. Finally he understood all too well. And this time, when his teeth bit deep into her tender flesh, her scream was loud enough to deafen the world. As the massively satisfying orgasm took control of her whole being, her body shook and shuddered, and wriggled and writhed, And still he held her in his merciless grip.

"Oh, thank God, thank God." At last it was over, and her relief was heavenly bliss. "I thought I was going to explode."

With her initial need satisfied they could take things a little slower. They both watched in the mirror again as his finger moved up and down between her moist labia. But it didn't last very long. She could feel his excitement. It was almost as if he was trembling inside and soon his slow gentle touch was scrambling her mind once more.

He had three fingers inside her now, moving slowly in and out and round and round. His finger found her clitoris, almost making her jump out of her seat with the shock of the massively increased sensation. She clutched his hand and looked at him with pleading eyes.

"Please!" She couldn't stand much more of this torment. She was almost crying with longing for him and he must enter her now.

"Come on."

He squeezed between the seats and helped her into the bay behind the curtains. She looked in amazement at the bed which had been right behind them all the time. She had had no idea that it was there, but what a marvellous idea. He lay back on top of the bedclothes with his head resting on the pillows. She scrambled quickly towards him, submissive, a slave on her knees. He sat up and pulled his shirt off over his head. He would have undone his belt as well, but she would have none of it; that was going to be her treat.

She pushed him back against the pillows and set to at once. She dragged his trousers off. Now he was wearing only ankle socks and jockey pants. And there was something very interesting lurking in those pants. She knelt and took off his right sock and carefully rolled it back on itself. Without taking her eyes from his she brought her right hand swiftly back against her left hand and sent the sock flying over her left shoulder. She dealt with the other sock in a similar manner. And that left only his underpants between her and her quarry. She lifted his leg and ducked under it then pulled both of his legs tight against hers so that they were as closed as they could be with her kneeling in between them.

She leant forward and put her fingers into the waist band on either side of his pants. Then with one swift movement she ripped them down, lifted his legs up and pulled his pants from his ankles.

She knelt in front of him, hot flushed and wild eyed, and took one of his balls in either hand, weighed them as if trying to choose between two prime plums. Then she placed her left hand at the base of his shaft below his balls and traced up the underside of his penis with the pointed nail of her right index finger.

"Oh my God!" Mario's voice sounded strangled as he struggled not to spend himself.

She continued to look into his eyes while her finger nail moved round under the overhang of his knob. Satisfied, her nail finished its inspection and withdrew. The heavy knob drew a circle in the air then returned to its position just above Mario's belly. His cock was hers now. She turned her full attention to it, moving her eyes and fingers all over it, inspecting every miner imperfection and picking off one or two loose hairs and pieces of fluff. She held the base of his shaft between the fingers of both hands. And those hands looked so small, barely big enough to cover his balls.

"I think he's lovely." She spoke to Mario, but her words seemed to be addressed to his cock.

She could wait no longer. Her head dipped down and that wonderful cock disappeared inside her mouth. Instantly, a shudder of recognition and relief ran through the length and breadth of her body.

She placed her teeth firmly round his shaft at the base of his glans and started to bite into the firm springy flesh. Men were very trusting. She released the pressure of her teeth and let his knob slip back out between her lips, sucking and licking him like a lollipop.

Then she took him between her breasts...

Suddenly she knew she had gone too far. She could see it in Mario's anguish and despair. And she could feel it in the heat and excitement of that lovely pulsating lump of flesh which she held so close to her heart. He came with a groan, wasting himself. The first massive plume of sperm coated her face with its heavy warm stickiness.

It was wonderful!

It was something she had always wanted to do, but it was much, much, better than she had ever imagined it would be. It was all sticky, and messy, and nice. And Mario's cock was magnificent, flexing and jerking between her breasts and ejaculating all over them and her face with an unending supply of beautiful thick spunk. She was squealing and giggling like a kid and when he was almost done she released him from his soft springy prison so that she could spread his wonderful spunk all over her breasts and face. When she was finished it felt as if she had it everywhere and the palms of her hands and between her fingers were all beautifully sticky with it.

At last she remembered poor Mario, and taking his cock in both hands she popped it in her mouth. Then she nursed him with her tongue, all the time stroking his balls, until she had made completely sure that she had milked every last drop out of him.

"There's a sink," he said, sternly now. He pointed down past his feet.

She wet a flannel and wiped his cock clean before dealing with herself.

She knew she was in trouble for making him come like that. He must consider it a great waste. She knelt in front of him between his legs and tried to calm herself down. But she didn't feel like being calm. What ever he did, she would still feel that it had been worth it. Anyway, some of it was his fault. He was her master, he should have stopped her.

"Fetch my belt."

That calmed her a little. "Master!" she pleaded.

"Now!"

Her fingers shook as she pulled the thick leather belt free of the loops. She had never been beaten very hard. She knew that even Margaret had been gentle with her when she had thrashed her with the carriage whip. Not that it had felt gentle at the time. But something told her that Mario could be cruel when he wanted to be. She hardly dared to look him in the eye as she handed him the belt.

"Not too hard, Master."

"Lie down."

She lay down with her head between his thighs and buried her face in the bedclothes. She took a mouthful of blanket as the belt whistled through the air and struck her on the right cheek of her bottom with a force that took her breath away. Almost before she could scream the second blow struck her on the other cheek. She began to twist and turn and scream for him to stop. And she couldn't stop herself, she had to cover her bottom with her hands. He lashed at her hands, and it hurt like buggery, but she didn't dare take them away.

He stopped, and she could tell from his voice that he was very angry.

"Move your hands."

"I can't! I can't! It hurts too much!"

"MOVE YOUR HANDS!"

172

Now she was sobbing helplessly into the blanket. She didn't want to disobey, but she just couldn't, surely he must understand that.

He left her for a moment and she knew that he had gone into the front of the cab. When he came back he dragged her up to the top of the bed and secured her arms to the bunk head with layers of canvas tape which he tore from a large roll.

Now it was his turn to be hot and flushed and wild eyed with hands which shook uncontrollably. She glanced at his cock as he pushed and shoved at her, forcing her into the position he wanted her in. It was huge. Big and purple, and stiff, like a rod of steel.

Now he began to beat her in earnest. She knew that he was out of control, but she didn't know what she could do about it. He stopped after a bit and taped up her mouth. His eyes were those of a maniac. His hands shook so much that it took him ages to catch her shaking head and apply the first strip of tape. And when she continued to struggle, twisting her head from side to side, he struck her across the face. By the time he had finished he was gasping for breath. He continued to sit at her head getting his breath back, so she was able to look at his cock. He looked at it himself. It had a long thin line of a thick clear liquid bubbling from it. He wiped it off with his hand, but it was immediately replaced with a new flow. He wiped his fingers on the blanket and moved away.

He started to beat her again, but this was different. He was in control again. His strokes were measured. And after giving her another three, he began to check with his hand between each stroke. As her excitement started to rise she began to wriggle and try to shout through her gag. But he didn't need her help to tell him when she was right on the edge.

He came and removed her gag, tearing it off in one swift movement. She was very close. He placed his lips in the small of her back and began to kiss his way down to her bottom. It was unbelievable. Her vagina felt as if it was weeping; melting into the mattress. She started to cry.

"What's the matter?"

"I love you, Master!"

He placed his hands on her shoulders and ran his fingers down either side of her body until they met at her toes. Then he kissed the soles of her feet.

"Please, Master, please."

"What?"

"Beat me again, Master, please, beat me again!"

He beat her then as she had never been beaten before. She came at once, with the first stroke, and she continued to come with every subsequent one. He nursed it all out of her, until she was a helpless sobbing wreck, then he threw the belt aside and released her hands. She jumped on him immediately, wrapping her arms around his neck and smothering his face with her tears in her anxiety to find his lips. They were like animals. He entered her immediately, with such force that he pushed her right across the bed and pinioned her against the wall.

Her legs were over the crooks of his arms and her bottom six inches from the mattress. And he thrust into as if he wanted to kill her. He was a maniac and a beast. He attacked her with a hatred which had no more finesse than his original onslaught with the belt. And he totally destroyed her with a dozen hard strokes. In the process, he totally destroyed himself as well. With the last stroke, she stopped crying and egging him on, and they stayed like that for an eternity, while her heart hammered against the wall of her chest with a violence which made her head throb with pain. Then he wrenched himself free and threw himself face down on the bed while she slid down the wall and back onto the bed. She sat there panting, watching his back rising and falling, and a large grin appeared on her face. She hurt everywhere, and if she could ever find the strength to get up, she wouldn't be able to sit down for a week. But, by God, had it been worth it!

Eventually he recovered enough to turn himself onto his back. He looked at her watching him and slowly he began to smile. It appeared that they were both pretty pleased with themselves.

"Which do you prefer then, gentle or hard?"

"I'll tell you when I've tried the hard."

"You, little bugger! Where's that belt?"

CHAPTER 17

He parked out in the lay-by.

Deep in the wood they came across a dozen large fallen trees which had been bulldozed into a heap to await removal - had he known they were there?

They had probably lain there for years; the last great hurricane must have torn them from the life giving earth. It was a strange magical place which gave her strange primitive thoughts.

He helped her climb into the centre of them, and once there, they were completely alone. It was like being in an elephant's graveyard, surrounded by those magnificent noble oaks which had lasted for five hundred years before being dashed to the ground in a minute. She felt strange, as if she had entered a cathedral. Nature's cathedral. Nature's own testimony to its own power. There was something pagan and primeval about that place. She could feel it in the air, and smell it, with every breath she took.

Of course, they weren't the first to have been there. Most of the grass had been kept short by the passage of feet. And there was evidence of old fires, and even previous love making. But they had it to themselves for now; a totally private area of about twenty square feet surrounded on all sides by six-foot-high walls of solid oak.

He gave her a moment to take it all in, then led her to the centre.

"Put on a show for me."

"What?"

He smiled and spread his arms wide as he turned full circle."Do whatever you think this place would like."

She realised that he felt it too, the strange power that the place had.

He walked off and sat down on one of the massive dead trunks. He looked at her expectantly as if anticipating a treat. She started to strip for him. It didn't take long, she only had the waistcoat and skirt. But by the time she had taken them off and was standing naked she knew that she wanted to turn him on. She desperately wanted to see him admiring her body and to know that he wanted her. She started to caress all over her own body imagining that she was performing for an audience and that it was their hands and arms that she could feel stroking her skin.

She placed her hands under her breasts, offering them to him as if they were ripe melons, then ran her fingers and the palms of her hands over their smooth firm roundness until her nipples were bullet hard. She took each nipple between finger and thumb and twisted them, trying to wind them up. Then she let them wind back, before twisting them in the other direction. She was excited now, and her eyes kept disappearing beneath her lids as she turned her face up towards the clear blue sky.

He was sitting on an upper trunk with one leg bent and the other stretched out straight with the foot just resting on the lower trunk. He took his hand and squeezed his erection as if trying to ease the ache in his balls. She pushed her breasts together and ran the two nipples over each other. It was no good, she could resist no longer. Her right hand went to her vagina and after making sure that her fingers were nicely wet, she found her clitoris with her index finger and started to rotate it round and round, keeping rhythm with the fingers on her nipple and the excitement rising inside her.

He unzipped his fly and took his cock out. He held it in the centre with his fingers underneath and his thumb on top, and jiggled it a couple of times. It didn't need any further encouragement. It stood up and turned its pink face towards her.

She desperately wanted to go on watching, but her eyes would no longer focus properly. She closed them and abandoned herself to her orgasm. At last it had happened. She was masturbating in front of a man. Letting him see all the expertise she had gained over all those lonely nights. She had imagined this so often. But her imagination had never done full justice to the reality. This was wonderful. This was heaven. Her fingers felt like old friends. And in her mind she imagined every man in the world masturbating over her. She felt the hot sperm hitting her skin, coating her from head to toe in its wonderful, thick, suffocating stickiness, until she could no longer move her limbs and was destined to remain cocooned in it for ever more.

This was different to every other time. This was what he wanted her to do. It was like having his permission to do what she had longed to do for so long. God, it was wonderful. She hadn't realised how much she had needed it. She was going faster and faster now and she wasn't going to be able to stand any longer. She bent her legs and eased herself to the ground; unable to stop her hypnotic caresses even while she sat herself down.

She bent forward. Her feet were apart: and her knees were together, with her forehead resting on them. It was going to be big. One of the greatest orgasms she had ever given herself. She forced her eyes open. He was staring at her. His eyes were bulging and his face was full of lust. He was almost there. She lay on her back thrusting her hips high in the air listening to her own animal grunts of satisfaction as she came. Again and again her hips thrust forward and back as she fucked her own hand, grunting and whimpering with the effort and the ecstasy of it. Christ, it had been so long and she had needed it so much.

From the corner of her eye she saw him let fly with his own ejaculation. And she cried out for both of them with a scream of triumph. She lay back on the grass. She was exultant. But also exhausted and content. She lay there, too tired to move, feeling the warm sunlight on her body, and she knew that she had a huge self-satisfied smile on her face. Possibly the biggest smile any face had ever worn. And why not? It must have been the biggest orgasm anyone had ever had!

She saw the shadow cross her eyelids and knew that he had come to stand over her. She opened her eyes and looked up at him. He was smiling down at her and she knew that she had pleased him. She returned his grin, feeling like the cat who had swallowed the cream. He had pleased her too. What she had just done had been perfect; so wicked, and so satisfying. How had he known? Was it obvious that she was an exhibitionist who enjoyed making love to herself? She hadn't known. But now that she did, it was so beautifully erotic that she knew she must do it again and again.

He offered her his hand and pulled her to her feet. She put her arms round his neck and he held her tight, kissing her on the forehead.

Then he carried her over to where he had been sitting and put her down while he took something from the back pocket of his slacks.

The trees must have stood fifty or sixty feet tall before they fell, with trunks too thick for her to have stretched her arms around. She watched as he knelt on one at the bottom of the pile and reached up to a branch on the one on top of it.

As the pink condom unwound over the gnarled knobbly surface, she realised that the end of the short branch had been carved so that it now resembled a hugely oversized penis. At the bottom of the branch some distortion of nature had created a large round bulge. It was just like a man's scrotum, only covered with a rough bark with a deeply indented pattern. There was no doubt about it, this was the dead tree's cock.

And she knew that she must fuck it!

There was something filthy and evil about her desire. But it was no good. It was a craving which wouldn't be denied. And she knew she would make love to that tree with every ounce of strength in her body.

She turned to look at him. What she saw in his face made her shudder with a mixture of horror and longing. He had brought her here to do this. He was a procurer. He had procured her body for the tree, and now he was going to watch it take his sacrifice. She turned back to look at the trunk. There was something dreadfully obscene about the sight of this once noble tree with its penis dressed in a thin pink rubber mask.

The condom didn't reach all the way to the bottom, and the branch was at least twice as thick as anything she had previously had inside her. Her whole body began to shake. She couldn't breathe and she felt almost giddy with excitement.

She had no idea how she got up there. She could feel his hands supporting her, on her bottom, and under her breasts, as he offered her up to the tree. The bark was cutting hard into her inner legs at the thighs, knees, and ankles, as she struggled to ensure that she didn't descend onto it too quickly.

"No!" she heard a distant voice squealing.

His hands were on her, supporting her weight, but he said nothing and made no effort to remove her. She wanted to struggle, or to look at him. She needed to verify that this what he really wanted; to give her to another. To allow her to make love to another while he watched. But she didn't dare look away, in case she did herself an injury with a sudden movement. The branch was between her inner labia, at the entrance to her vagina. He must stop. He must realise that it was too big.

"Stop it! He's too big!" She heard the little girl screaming again.

She wiggled in his grip, trying to resist. She screamed as the pressure became unbearable. Then all at once, it slipped inside. It took her breath away. She clenched her teeth and groaned. It was so big. It was splitting her in half. She could feel it breaking the bone and tearing the skin. She was going to die, impaled on this branch.

"Please! Please! Oh God!" Her voice was an agonised croak, without the power to make itself heard.

Slowly the branch continued on its way, slipping further and further inside and she didn't die. She forgot everything in her effort to accommodate it. The sensation in her body was incredible. She was so full and tight there was no room for anything else. It was pressing right up against her spine paralysing her. Then she knew that he couldn't get it out. It would never come out, this was the end. But what an end!

Her hands were just in front of her vulva with her palms pressed hard against the bark trying to support her weight. She leant forward with her arms coming straight down from her shoulders. Then she slowly bent them until her breasts touched the rough surface of the bark, followed by her forehead. Her legs were behind her, bent at the knee with the ankles on the log behind her and her weight resting on her bent toes. She moved her legs round until they were at ninety degrees to the rest of her body. The tree trunk was so thick that her legs were splayed out sideways as if she was riding a grossly overweight donkey. Now there wasn't anything she could do to stop the tree from penetrating her. Only the human hands supporting her weight prevented the trunk from shooting up and spearing her insides.

Slowly the branch entered her until the tree possessed her completely. She felt her clitoris contact the rough bark on the hump at the bottom of the branch and her mouth opened into a silent scream which she turned into a kiss of gratitude.

The human left her then. She didn't know where he went, but she knew that she was alone. Just herself and the tree. The tree's rough skin was touching her everywhere. It bit into her: forehead, lips, breasts, belly, thighs, knees, and ankles. And it was inside her; huge and demanding. It was as if they were one. The tree was her new lover who she must worship. She started to shake with the start of her first orgasm. She was being fucked by a tree and the sensation was incredible.

Then she _felt_ human hands on her again.

They travelled slowly down her spine from her shoulders to her bottom. And, at last, as they did so, they seemed to ease the pressure inside her so that she didn't feel quite so stretched. They arrived at her bottom and slowly caressed round and round her cheeks. Then one of them stroked up the cleft of her bum and she jumped at the contact and started to orgasm again.

"Ahhhhh!"

She jumped so hard with the first blow from the belt that she was certain she had ruptured herself. Her entire body was instantly covered with a film of sweat and her burning skin was so sensitive that she could even feel the still air rushing across its surface. The second stroke was worse. She was as tight as a drum, inside and out, and she had no strength left to cope with any additional stimulus. She thought she must die with the third stroke. She knew she would rupture her insides if she jumped so hard, spearing herself on the branch with her descent, but there was no way she could stop.

Then, with the fourth stroke, her orgasm took over and she no longer had any concern for the consequences. Now she belonged to him and would continue to react to the blows from the belt whatever happened. She was an animal without a brain or identity. She didn't know what she was, or who she was, or her purpose in the scheme of things. The belt cracked against her skin, burning the cheeks of her bottom with a thin strip of white hot pain, and she re-acted, lifting herself up on the branch which lived inside her. Her breasts rubbed against the rough bark bringing a different pain to her nipples. A harsher pain which was almost a relief.

She screamed and gasped for air, and descended again feeling the massive alien entity inside her squeezing her apart. The belt hit her again and again and again and soon her whole world belonged to this thing which lived inside her. And she rose and descended on it, reacting to the belt's demands. It couldn't move. But that didn't matter. In fact it was good. She didn't want it to. She would do the moving for both of them. That was what she wanted. She wanted to do the fucking. She wanted to drive her body against this dead monster while the remorseless belt whipped her and drove her on to greater and greater madness.

She could hear the squelching as the branch slid up and down inside her. And she gradually grew to know every one of its lumps and bumps until it became an old and fa-miliar friend who she wanted to please. The rhythm of the belt grew more urgent and she started to whimper and cry out in frustration and despair as she struggled to keep pace with its demands.

She was breathless now and fast reaching her climax and the end of her last reserves of power. Suddenly he was there, even deeper, penetrating to her full extent. She had no more to give. He had taken every part of her. She was forced to lift herself off the tree, throwing her head back and arching her spine, and deep inside her body made another quarter of an inch of room and she forced herself down even further determined to take everything that it had to offer. Nothing had ever been this far inside her before.

She was taking a terrible chance; any further and she would be dead. She had at last given everything and felt a lover as far inside as he could get. For a moment the world stopped still. She was fulfilled, her purpose in life achieved. Her lover had penetrated as deep as he could go and now he must fertilise her. But nothing happened and she started to franticly ride him again, lifting her thighs high in the air then grinding them down again against his rough surface.

At last she lay against the tree trunk, completely limp and totally exhausted. She had no strength left to lift her weight from him at all now. She hugged him and felt his rough old body biting into her soft young flesh. She had made love to a tree. Her tree. Was there anything more decadent? Could she fall any lower? Was there nothing she would deny herself to achieve sexual gratification? She chastised herself for her wantonness, but all the time as she did so, there was another little voice at the back of her mind and it reminded her of how good it had felt to be penetrated all the way, so deep that her legs were paralysed and his knob felt as if it was buried behind her burning breasts.

It was wonderful to feel human arms round her with his hands on her breasts and his cheek in the small of her back, but she could hardly believe it when she felt his penis at the entrance to her anus. Surely he must realise that there was no room left inside her for him?

Slowly he pressed closer. She had no strength to stop him. She had no strength at all. But he would never get inside. She was already full. She tried to ignore what he was trying to do and concentrate on how lovely it was to feel arms round her and the warmth of a living body against hers, in contrast to the harsh indifference of the tree as it pressed hard against her soft flesh.

But the human penis was large in the cleft of her bottom and it was warm and alive and throbbing with the pulse of life. And she wanted it inside.

Now the throbbing thing slipped inside and she cried out in shock and pleasure. Oh, it was wonderful, and where the knob could enter surely the rest could follow? She had never felt like this before. It was as if they were one. Slowly it slid forward, but the tree opposed it all the way, and it was held up for minutes at a time while the pressure built up enough to allow it to climb up over the lumps and bumps of his nobly companion and slide down the other side. Now that the human lover was under way he was as unstoppable as a juggernaut moving relentlessly onwards a fraction at a time.

Her mouth, eyes, and ears were forced wide open as she struggled to survive the battle which raged inside her. They were alone in this place, but she could hear every sound. She could clearly hear the rushing of the air and the swaying of the grass; the munching of the ladybird devouring a greenfly up above and the rasping sound of the field mouse cleaning his whiskers in his burrow beneath.

Her mouth was full of the bitter taste the pieces of bark on her teeth and tongue where she had bitten into the tree to help contain the pain of her ecstasy. The fallen tree smelt warm from the sun on its surface and the dust way down in the cracks in its bark where she could see the minute creatures that lived there. They moved about like tiny figures at the bottom of the Grand Canyon. What they were she had no idea. They were so minute that she could be the first person who had ever seen them. Perhaps she should give them a name to record that she was the person who had discovered them?

The penis arrived at its destination and could go no further. Her heart ached now from beating so hard for far too long. She felt weak and sick from its incessant bumping in her chest where it had swollen up until it blocked her lungs and made every breath a painful effort. Each time it beat, the pain travelled up her back and neck and thumped into the sore spongy spot deep inside the back of her head. It wasn't her heart's fault, it was keeping time with the beating pulse of the penis and had no choice in the matter, but she prayed for it to stop before she was too ill to carry on.

Now the penis started to move, and every part of her moved with it. They were one, and every part of her body swayed back and forth with every movement it made. It started to go faster and faster, pressing her hard against its rival as it ran back and forth over lumps and bumps.

The two monsters were separated by a thin membrane of her flesh. Soft, weak, sensitive flesh, which could be rubbed away or penetrated in an instant.

Her body started to make a whining scream which grew and grew. And every part of her was shaking. She was filled with a terrible fear and inevitability which continued to grow in intensity. She felt as if she was standing in the pitch black interior of a tunnel, listening to the terrible thundering of an approaching train. She knew she ought to flee; to try to save herself. But she couldn't. Her feet were rooted to the spot and she could do nothing but wait in horror. She was being shaken apart by the dreadful vibration of its approach. And all the time the scream was rising in her. It started from her stomach, rushed through her chest, and up into her throat. Then it escaped through her mouth and nose as a terrified whining shriek which grew ever louder.

The human was filled with more power than any man had ever possessed before. And when he came her world erupted. There was no space left inside her, but as he expanded and pumped out his white hot fire, she stopped screaming. The sudden silence was far worse than the terrifying noise it replaced. Then suddenly her shriek returned, more blood curdling than ever. Her anus tried to squeeze him so tight that he wouldn't be able to move again, but he was too strong for her and he wouldn't be denied. Her iron grip was thrust aside as hot juices jetted into her furthest reaches. Each time she gripped him and each time he broke free to come again and fill her narrow passage with squelching juices.

At last, as the human's strength started to fade, she was able to move for them both and all at once she was coming herself, with a climax which was as violent and as satisfying as her scream. The last echo of that terrible sound faded. The terrified creatures stopped crouching in fear and their hearts started beating again. And she knew that, at long last, she must have experienced the ultimate ecstasy. Surely, no better moment existed this side of heaven? The penis continued to move up and down inside her for several more minutes. But it was a slowing down now, like the slowing paces of an exhausted runner after the finish of a race. His exhaustion pleads with him to stop, but the rhythm of his body demands a gentle decline. And the rhythm of her body pleaded with him not to stop. It was ecstasy. An ecstasy which was almost too great to endure. She shook her head from side to side, trying to find a way to cope with the splendour of this fading glory.

She slept all the way home; curled up in a little ball in the passenger seat: so tight that her legs were completely hidden under the tiny skirt. She didn't dream, but she had a smile on her face which reflected the contentment in her heart.

She was with the most wonderful man she knew. She loved her true master; she always would. But he was gone now. She would never see him again. And this man, the one she belonged to now, had given her the best day of her life.

She was his for ever, and he was hers.

For ever.

CHAPTER 18

She awoke when the lorry stopped. Her eyes slowly opened and his smiling face was there to welcome her back.

"Where are we?"

"Home. Your new home. Do you want to see?"

She nodded and he left her. She was still too lazy to move and she knew that he would come and lift her down. She leant against the side of the lorry while he insisted on crouching down and putting her shoes on. It was nice to feel the touch of his hands on her legs and see his look of pride as he smoothed her crumpled waistcoat and made sure that she was presentable. But she was impatient for a cuddle and a kiss and she knew that they would only take them off again once they were inside.

She clung to him, moving unsteadily on her high heels, and making his life difficult as he struggled to unlock the door. He didn't bother with the electric light in the hallway. They crossed it in the near dark using the dim dusk light shining through the windows to illuminate their way to a room on the far side. This time he did use the electric light. He stopped just inside the doorway and flicked the switch. Half a dozen mellow wall lights came on to dimly illuminate a cosy old-fashioned room crowded with big heavy furniture.

The flock wallpaper, drapes, ornaments, and abundance of framed pictures, gave the room a Victorian feel. In fact, she was willing to bet that it was more or less authentic, and hadn't changed much for many many years. She liked it and immediately felt at home in it. She moved to the centre of the room and turned slowly round, taking it all in before turning back to look at him with a smile of approval.

He was looking over her shoulder and she turned to see why. A dark man with shiny, slicked-back, black hair, was standing looking at her with a superior smile on his face. He must have been there in the room all the time, sitting in one of the deep armchairs, waiting for them in the dark. And she must have looked straight through him as she inspected the room.

"This is my older brother, Georgio - your new master."

She didn't understand. She swung round and stared at Mario. He shrugged his shoulders and laughed. "I was just the messenger boy, but it was fun."

She turned back to Georgio. He was smiling as well. But it wasn't from kindness, or sympathy. There was terrible cruelty in those eyes. She pitied anyone who came under his control. She shuddered at the thought. Mario brushed past her and handed Georgio the small leather pouch. He turned and winked at her as he made his way back towards the door.

"Well, good night you two. Have fun."

She watched the door closing on him. She wanted to run after him; tell him that he couldn't leave her here with this terrifying man.

"Sit."

She turned back to him. Every movement was reluctant, and that fact wasn't wasted on him. He motioned her to one of the over stuffed armchairs. He behaved as if she was an honoured guest in his home who must be treated with every courtesy. She shook her head, trying to remain calm.

"I want to go please."

He opened the wallet and inspected the contract. He looked at her when he had finished. She knew what he was thinking. There was nothing she could do about it. She belonged to him completely. Her only escape was death.

"A very impressive document."

She nodded her agreement.

"All my own work."

What did he mean? Had she been intended for him all along? Had her real master accepted her as a slave knowing that he was going to pass her on to this frightening monster?

He was opening the letter now. It made him smile. "Your previous master recommends that you be beaten every day."

She felt cold. The room was hot. Much too hot. But she was suddenly ice cold. "I-I-I don't think that's necessary any more. I have learnt my lesson. I- I- I know how to be a good girl now. I think that must have been written before."

She closed her eyes at the shame of her stutter. Why did she have to make it so easy for people to despise her and make fun of her? No wonder they thought her a fool and didn't want to be her friend.

"It's dated yesterday."

"Oh." Her response sounded dull and full of resignation. And why not? She had done her very best for her true master. He had said as much. He had said that she had done well. He had said that she was obedient. But now she found that he still believed that she needed to be disciplined every day.

Georgio walked over to the matching armchair and took something from a tall narrow vase at its side. She saw that it was some sort of cane. He held it between his hands and stroked it lovingly as he brought it back for her to see. It was obviously a prized possession. He handed it to her so that she could inspect it. The handle was made of ivory and looked very old. It had been expertly carved into a representation of a hideous squat Chinese who also had the shape and size of a nine inch penis.

In one hand, the figure in the carving held the severed head of a beautiful young woman. She was hanging from her own long hair, with eyes closed, serene in death. Her expression contrasted shockingly with the awful manic stare of the carving, which showed the pride the Chinaman had in his gruesome possession. Except for the wide circular hat he was completely naked and the front of his body was dominated by a massively oversized erection which reached almost up to his chin. For some reason he was standing on the back of a dragon with a curved tail. Its evil stare was almost as horrifying as his own.

Emerging from the hilt of the handle were six strips of split cane.

They were each thirty inches long and had been individually polished and varnished. Each of them was etched with Chinese characters in red ink.

Susan started to shudder.

She pressed her index finger against the dragon's tail. It felt like a sharp claw which would tear at her flesh. And it was perfectly designed to make contact with her clitoris each time that the hideous little image thrust in and out of her. She looked up at Georgio, her face contorted into a look of abject terror. It was what he wanted; what he had intended. And, as he bent and took the cane from her shaking fingers, his own face betrayed his quiet satisfaction.

He returned to his chair and waited for her to speak. But she couldn't. This evil man was going to flay her alive with that disgusting instrument of torture, and she must let him. She was completely alone and helpless to do anything about it.

"How old are you?"

"Twen-t-ty-t-two. Twenty-two." Her voice faltered as she stammered over her reply to his simple question.

"What did you call your other master?"

She understood. There was no need for him to say anything more. "Master, Master."

He nodded with satisfaction.

"You look far younger. In this light you barely look more than a child."

"I'm sorry, Master."

"Don't be. It wasn't a complaint."

He was quiet, lying back in his chair and looking into the glowing red embers of the fire. Susan turned to look at them too. Even though it must now be completely dark outside, it wasn't a cold night, and the fire was more for show than warmth. She looked at the pictures in the jumping flames and somehow the usually comforting sight made his menacing evil seem all the worse.

"Sometimes little girls are naughty and then they have to be punished."

Susan looked at him, but he was speaking to the fire.

"Have you been naughty?"

What was the answer? What did he want to hear? She didn't want him to beat her with that terrible cane. "Yes, Master," she heard a little-girl voice say. "I made love to a tree!"

"Come to me."

Her heart jumped and she was incapable of movement. She continued to stare at him, petrified by her fear.

He turned to look at her.

"Come to me." His voice was soft and gentle, but his command wasn't to be ignored for a second time.

She rose and somehow walked the few steps until she was standing facing him a couple of feet in front of his chair. He looked at her for some time, saying nothing, his expression giving nothing away. Then he rose and walked past her and she heard him stoking the fire and felt the increased heat on the back of her legs. He came and sat down again.

"Undress."

Her fingers fumbled with the buttons on her waistcoat. Luckily they were reasonably large and heart shaped and her clumsy fingers were able to grip them and force them through the buttonholes. She took the waistcoat off and held it in one hand waiting for his instruction. But he made no indication where she should put it and she let it drop to the floor.

The flickering fire was burning the skin on her back and she felt faint from the sudden increase in heat. Her knees were bent and she was too weak to straighten them. Her fingers couldn't open the buckle of her belt. She was almost hysterical now, certain that he would loose patience with her, but he remained calm and eventually her bruised fingers forced it open. She pulled the belt apart and let her skirt drop away. She could feel it round her ankles. And now the fire was burning her bare bum and drying the juices on her inner thighs.

"Are you too hot?"

She nodded. She could hardly stand the burning heat.

He had the cane in his right hand and he used it to indicate that she should move to her left away from the fire. Her heels caught in her skirt almost causing her to fall. She gave a little cry and realised that she wasn't far from tears. She kicked the skirt free and moved to where he wanted her. When she had done so, he pulled his chair round slightly on the casters, so that once more she was standing directly ahead of him. He looked at her for some time.

"Turn round."

She felt his eyes on her back and wondered how her anus must look. She could feel that her labia hadn't returned inside her body since their encounter with the branch. Would her anus betray the evidence of penetration in a similar way? Her clitoris felt as long as a babies thumb and she could tell from the heat of the fire on it that it was standing completely proud of its protective hood. Her hands longed to touch it and they fidgeted nervously at her side as she fought an internal battle to control them.

He placed the cane at the nape of her neck, just below her hair, and as he ran it slowly down her spine, her entire body shuddered. It reached the cleft between the cheeks of her bottom and as it approached her anus, her knees gave way and buckled for a moment before she recovered. He placed the cane on the outside of her right thigh and pressed.

"Turn."

She turned to the side. He placed the cane on her belly and pressed. She turned again so that she was facing him again. The cane started at her neck and traced its way down to her pubic mound. She felt her juices trickle out and moisten her outer labia and she bit her lip trying not to cry out. It returned to the crest of her right breast and moved down until it was on her aureola. It circled round, pressing on harder and suddenly her breath was taken away as it gripped her nipple.

How it was done she didn't know, but her nipple was held tight in the very centre of its six slithers of bamboo. They held it there, in a steel grip as if it was being held by a tiny claw. He turned the cane between finger and thumb and her legs gave way completely allowing her to crumple to the floor.

She was his now. The slightest movement of the cane made her draw in her breath, bite her lip and wriggle her body.

"Do you want to use your fingers?"

She opened her eyes and looked at her evil tormentor. He despised her for what she was and he wanted to prove how weak and wanton she was. She must say no and prove that he was wrong. What he wanted her to do was obscene and degrading and done from hate, not love.

She nodded her head. Her eyes wouldn't close now. She must watch her own humiliation in his eyes. Her fingers found her clitoris and started the old familiar caress. Her clitoris had never been this big before, or more demanding and she needed both hands to satisfy it. The pain in her neck was horrendous, and her eyeballs desperately wanted to disappear behind the lids of her wildly staring eyes, but she wouldn't let them. She wouldn't allow herself to miss even a split second of her own degradation.

She was almost there. Her breath was coming in great gasps and her fingers were moving ever faster, and pressing ever harder. The cane was ripped from her nipple sending a shock wave through her which almost toppled her over the edge into climax. Then it cut across the knuckles of her right hand and even before she could give voice to her agony, it had done the same on her left hand. Her hands were on fire, and her fingers completely numb and useless. She began throwing herself about the floor trying to find some way of gaining relief from the horrendous pain.

Eventually she stopped moving and screaming. She lay on her stomach trying to force both hands into her mouth at the same time. Her mouth was full of the taste of her own juices and of the white hot skin of her fingers. She could smell the dust in the Axminster carpet, and see the widening dark circles in its complicated pattern as her tears continued to wet it. Suddenly she felt the cane on her bottom, cutting into the soft rounded mound of her right cheek. Her heart leapt and filled her throat once more as she realised that he was going to thrash her to a climax with that terrible cane.

The cane descended again and again and everywhere it went was turned to fire. She climaxed after the first few strokes, but he continued beating her on the bottom, thighs, and upper legs as far down as the back of her knees. She didn't try to resist the feeling inside her and she climaxed again and again, every few seconds. It was a nightmare, and a heavenly euphoria. She ground her clitoris hard against the carpet each time that the cane gave her time to do so. Then jumped with every part of her body as each new stroke struck her.

She scrambled round perversely trying to move her poor body beyond the reach of the cane which was bringing her such ecstatic delight. She was sure that the thick soft pile of the carpet was rubbing the skin from her shoulders, elbows, thighs, and knees. But she had no time to bother about that. She couldn't stop herself from wriggling and writhing as the cane continued to lead her rapturous squirming gyrations. She turned over, unable to stand any more stokes on her back and he hit her on her thighs, stomach, and breasts. None of the strokes were hard, but they delivered a sharp cutting pain which faded to a deep penetrating hum throughout her body.

She couldn't go on. She was exhausted. She couldn't continue the orgasm any longer or move her body at all.

His cane took her nipples again, twisting more emotion back into her ravaged body, then it snaked across her stomach and pubic mound as it made its way to her clitoris. She realised where it was going and opened her eyes wide in disbelief. It took her swollen clitoris and gripped it tight between its six little fingers.

She couldn't scream, or move. She couldn't close her eyes, or breath, or think. He held her whole world and her full concentration. Her mind was fully focused on thoughts of female circumcision as she waited to see what would happen. He twisted the cane gently round and then relaxed. He could do her such dreadful damage and give her such horrendous pain, but he wouldn't. He wanted to make her come as she had never come before.

And she wanted him to.

Afterwards.

A lifetime afterwards.

When he had taught her that she was helpless to deny him anything.

They remained in that cosy quiet room with the firelight flickering on the walls and ceiling and he made love to her again with his cane. She still lay on her back on the carpet while he sat in his comfortable chair. The only sounds were the ticking of the clocks, the beating of her heart, the rasping sound of her breath, and the squelching of the little Chinaman as he scurried hypnotically back and forth in and out of her body. He lifted her higher and higher, until she was floating on the white fluffy clouds and all the world was filled with love and kindness. Every now and then she opened her eyes. She knew he hadn't gone away, she just needed to look at that cruel handsome face with the gentle brown eyes.

There was no climax. The cane slipped from her and the next moment she was on his lap and in the safety of his strong protective arms.

"Hold me tight, Master, hold me tight."

He squeezed her until she couldn't breath, and when he relaxed, she started to cry with love for him and shame for herself. He was a monster, but she would serve him for the rest of her days, and give her thanks to God every night for sending her to him.

CHAPTER 19

When she awoke, she was still in Georgio's arms. She struggled to remember where she was. Then smiled in recognition. She had no idea what time it was. The lights were still on and the curtains closed, but she thought she could hear bird song. She looked at one of the clocks. Then confirmed the time with another. Almost five o'clock. In a little over an hour it would be a full day since she had left her true master. It felt like two lifetimes.

He stood up and put her down in the chair. His leg had gone to sleep and he hobbled up and down rubbing it until the life slowly returned to it. Then he made his way over to the fireplace and pulled the sash of a bell. She heard no sound, but after a few moments there was a knock at the door and she heard someone enter. Georgio was beating at the almost dead embers with the poker. He turned and looked over his shoulder, then stood up and turned to face into the room.

"This is Jerez, go with him."

Before she could move a man came from behind the chair and stood looking down at her. He was probably as tall as she was, but he looked far shorter. He was bowed down by a hunch back and his left arm was hanging loosely at his side. It seemed too long to be human and it hung down to his knee like that of an ape. He looked like Quasimodo. She ought to have felt like laughing, but she didn't. No one would have done once they had seen his face. His eyes were grey and penetrating like those of a hawk. And that was how the rest of his face looked. Sharp and bird like with a large hooked nose. The centre of his head was bald, but he wore the rest of his hair long and straight so that it reached down to his shoulders. It had probably been black once, but that was long ago. She was uncertain of his age, but judged him to be at least sixty.

He didn't seem to be at all surprised by her nudity, but she was suddenly very conscious of it. She tried to cover her breasts and force herself further back into the chair. He gave no reaction. He merely stood impassively waiting. She could hear Georgio still working on the fire; putting on new logs and coal. Then the sounds ceased and she jumped up quickly. He had just risen from the fire and was looking back into the room to see what was causing the delay. She hurried from the room before he made up his mind to be annoyed.

Jerez indicated the stairs and she started up them ahead of him. He followed her up and each step was an agony. She knew that he was just behind her gazing at her nakedness. She imagined how her bottom must look and her bare vulva. What did he think of her? What did he think of the angry red stripes which covered her body? They reached a half-landing with a single door, but he said nothing and she continued on. If only he weren't so quiet. If only he would make breathing noises, or say something.

"Stop."

She stopped on the landing.

"In there." He indicated the door at the far end.

It was a large bathroom, with grey marble walls, potted palms, and beautiful coloured sunlight streaming through the large stained glass windows. He walked over to the bath and set the taps running. She glanced self-consciously towards the lavatory.

"You can use the one in there." He indicated a connecting door and she gratefully took him up on his offer. When she returned her bath was almost ready. It looked very welcoming. The surface was a foot thick with foam and the air was thick with steam. She looked at herself in the many mirrors. At least six images of herself stared back at her. She could also see as many images of Jerez. This wasn't the room to spend a lot of time in if you looked like him. Frightening as he was, she suddenly felt very sorry for him. She looked at her own poor misused body in the nearest mirror. It was quite a shock. She really needed the comfort of that bath. She looked over at him. He took the thermometer from the water and nodded to her. It was ready.

She walked over. The bath was deep, with high sides. Presumably there were some steps somewhere. She began to look round for them, but he scooped her up and lifted her over the steaming water. He waited. And slowly she realised that she was perfectly safe. He must be incredibly strong to be able to remain there bent over the water supporting her weight. She looked into those hawk like eyes. He was in no discomfort. He could hold her suspended here all day. She looked away and dipped her toe into the water. It was perfect. Her foot followed and he gently lowered her down. She had never entered a bath like this before, not since she was a child.

"Relax and enjoy it, I'll be back to bathe you later."

What did he mean? She looked quickly round, the question on her lips, but he had already gone. And she quickly forgot it. The hot water made her flesh burn where it had been whipped, but it was comforting, like a balm. Now she realised how much her body ached and just how tired she was. She closed her eyes, and the next moment she felt the comfort of the water's gentle caress, and something else. She must have drifted off, because he had returned unheard, and was already bathing her.

His hands and the soap and flannel moved over her, and everywhere he went felt relaxed. This was wrong. This was decadent, to be washed by a servant. But everybody should try it at least once. His hands moved over her breasts. Then down over her stomach and round her waist. And finally to her waiting vulva. His fingers went inside her vagina, then moved on to wash her legs while her shocked mind tried to cope with the knowledge of his intimacy. He turned her over and made her kneel while he cleaned her bottom and back. Then he turned her onto her back once more and told her to sleep again.

By the time he had returned to lift her out and dry her down with large fluffy towels she felt ready to sleep for a week. So she didn't protest at all when he carried her to the bedroom and tucked her up in a huge four-poster bed.

"Wake up."

She opened her eyes and looked round at the unfamiliar surroundings. The lights were full on and she was lying naked in a large bed. She remembered that Jerez had put her in it. The covers had been thrown back and she could see herself clearly in the mirrored ceiling of the bed. The pillows were hardly creased and she was still lying where he had put her. She must have slept like a log.

"Sit up."

She did so, and for the first time looked at Jerez. She gasped, unable to believe what her eyes showed her. Instinctively she raised her legs and shuffled up the bed until the silken quilt headboard ensured that she could go no further. Jerez was naked. If a man like him could ever be naked. Every part of his body, except his penis and his hands and feet were covered with thick hair. He looked as hairy as an animal. And his penis looked like it belonged to one. It was over a foot long, and hung big, round, smooth, and heavy between his legs.

He sat on the bed, looking at her. Then he reached out and parted her knees. His hand slid down her leg to her inner thigh and began to stroke it.

"What are you doing?"

He ignored her question. "Are you hungry?"

She suddenly realised that she was and that was what the pain in her stomach meant. It felt like cramp. She must be famished.

"Yes."

"When did you last eat?"

"I don't know." It was hard to think with his hand on her body. She almost groaned aloud as she realised that her body was responding to him. Her nipples and clitoris were erect. Her labia were swollen and she could feel them becoming wet. "It was breakfast. I suppose it must have been about seven o'clock."

"That was the day before yesterday."

Was that possible? Could she have slept the clock round? "We'll eat afterwards. I'll cook us a banquet. Would you like that?"

"After what? What are you going to do?"

"You have to be beaten every day. And you've missed a day. We will have to beat you twice as much to make up."

"No! That's not up to you. I belong to your master."

"Not any more." He pulled at a cord which he had round his neck. It had lain completely buried by his body fur, but when he pulled it round she saw the leather wallet with her initials on. The golden letters danced before her eyes, growing larger and changing shape as they mocked her tears.

"No! I won't." She tried to scramble away from him, to leave the bed by the other side. But he caught hold of her wrist and slid her back. They looked at each other. She tried to be defiant, but how could she. How could anyone look into those unblinking grey eyes. She dropped her gaze, and he released her wrist and struck her on the cheek with the back of his hand. It wasn't a hard slap. It didn't have to be. She lay on her stomach biting the pillow and crying. He dragged her to the centre of the bed and placed a pillow under her belly. Then he tied her wrists and ankles with long silk cords.

He used a leather whip to beat her with. It had six wide leather thongs which splayed out to do the work of several whips. It didn't take long for him to make her come. When she started to orgasm he stopped.

"Shall I stop?"

"No! Don't stop, don't stop. Please, Jerez, beat me!"

"How shall I beat you?"

"Any way you please! Do anything, but just beat me!"

"And what shall I get for all my hard work?"

"Anything! You can have anything. I'll do anything you want."

He began beating her again. And now it wasn't just on the bottom. The whip ranged up her back and down her legs. Then he beat her on the soles of the feet until even she couldn't stand it.

She lay sobbing, and shaking like an hopeless jelly while he threw off her bonds. Then he turned her on her back and dragged her to the edge of the bed. She lay with her head hanging over the edge looking up at that giant penis. It was only partly erect with the knob dangling down towards her. He teased her, bending his knees and letting it bob into one eye then the other. Then he laughed as he used it to trace all over her face as she chased after it with her open mouth. At last he let her capture it and drag it inside. He moved his hands to her breasts and within seconds his monster was firm and fat.

He squeezed her nipples between fingers and thumbs, making her scream and eject his manhood from her mouth.

"Plead with me, tell me you want me."

"Please, Jerez, don't play games, I can't last any longer, I must have you, Please, please."

He moved his hands to either side of her waist and put his cock back into her mouth. Then he thrust forward. There was no teasing now. And no more holding back as he shagged her throat like a man demented. When he had finished with her, he left her crying and choking with his sperm coming from her mouth and nostrils. But only for a moment while he climbed up to join her. Then he dragged her to the centre of the bed and climbed on top of her. She looked up into the mirrors. Her face was covered with sperm and a hump-backed hairy beast was on top of her, thrashing away at her as if he intended to tear her to pieces.

She closed her legs round his hairy body and linked her ankles. He drove into her like a maniac, until she couldn't move. It hurt like buggery. Even with a normal sized weapon, with that much force, it must bring great pain. But she knew that he needed it. She knew that he needed to hurt her, and she wanted him to.

Then he threw her on her stomach, lifted up her hips and inserted himself into her anus. He took her then as it should be done. As animals should do it. She watched in the angled mirror above the headboard. It wasn't possible for it to get any more erotic than this. The single mirror carried the reflection from the overhead mirrors. so looking into it she could see it all. She could see her own bottom, with his massive shaft disappearing inside it then reappearing again, all purple and slimy. And she could see his hands on her breasts, digging into them with his claws. And she could see his deformed body and piercing eyes, and her own agonised expression with her mouth open wide by constant screams.

He stayed with her for several hours, beating her and screwing her. Before it happened she wouldn't have believed that one man could have so much energy and that she could take so much pain. And she wouldn't have believed that one man could be so kind and so cruel. In between his almost total moments of selfish madness, he cuddled her, cradling her in her arms and reigning kisses on her as he repeated his love for her over and over again. He took her to the bathroom several times and washed her in the shower, before carrying her back to the bed and kissing every inch of her body. Then he beat her mercilessly again until her own desires were once more aroused.

When he had finished, she slept again while he prepared the meal. Then they had a picnic in the middle of the huge bed. At last she could eat no more. She lay back against the pillows and looked at him sitting cross-legged, surrounded by the remainder of their meal, sipping champagne from a crystal glass. He looked like a young boy instead of a man of sixty. It was strange how nature has a way of compensating for the sick jokes she plays on people. Most people would have considered Jerez to be deformed and ugly. Certainly he did. But looking at him now, he was beautiful. Nature had equipped him to be her almost perfect lover. She didn't love him. She could never love anyone but her true master. But she would enjoy living with him and being his slave.

On the evening Jerez bathed her again as he had before.

"How do you feel now?"

"Wonderful! But I don't think I could make love again. Ever!

He laughed. "I'm not surprised, three men in three days, and one of those you spent sleeping."

That made her think of something which had been gnawing at her brain. "It's not quite three is it. Your master didn't actually make love to me did he?"

"I suppose not, if you look at it that way."

"Why not? Why did I displease him."

"Don't worry, little one, you didn't."

"But you said..."

"I know what I said. It wasn't strictly true. Georgio can't make love that way. Not the way you mean."

"Oh, I'm sorry!"

"Georgio can satisfy a woman. There's no doubt about that. Except in his own mind. That's why he keeps me. Together we make a whole man." He laughed, "Sort of."

"Don't, Jerez. You have nothing to be ashamed of, you're beautiful."

"Thank you, my pet. I know I am." He laughed again. "But you see, because Georgio can't satisfy a woman that way, he thinks it's important. He thinks that all women must want that. So he likes to watch, while I do it for him."

It took Susan a moment to realise what he meant. Then as realisation dawned he nodded.

"All those mirrors you mean?"

"That's it."

She looked round at all the mirrors which surrounded them.

"Yes," Jerez confirmed her unvoiced suspicions. "Almost every mirror in this part of the house.

"And can he hear us? Is he listening to us now?" she asked, sitting up in sudden panic.

"He could, except he's not here. But he'll be back soon. He has something to say to you so we'll have to dress you up properly. Not in that awful stuff you arrived in. He never wants to see you dressed like that again. Neither do I. I've thrown it out."

"I'm sorry, Jerez." Then suddenly as she thought of what he'd said. "What have you got for me."

"Ah, just like a woman. You'll have to wait, you little monkey. Let's get you all nice and clean first."

She stood in front of the long mirror in the bedroom and looked at herself. The dress was nothing too fancy, but she loved it. It was practical too. It was full length to her ankles. It had a shirt collar and sleeves, buttons all down the front, and a belt at the waist. It was in beige wool, and she had a pair of beige shoes to go with it. Again the heels were high, but this time they were wedges and much more comfortable to wear and walk on. Jerez buttoned it for her, doing up every one of the ten large bone buttons. Then he examined her and undid the very top one.

"Walk in it."

She walked along the wall of mirrored doors. She could hardly believe the image they showed her of herself. She looked so elegant and grown-up. The dress restricted the movement of her legs, making her take much shorter steps. With each movement it was pulled tight against different parts of her body, making the eye naturally turn to examine them. It was almost as if it was holding her in bonds from which her body was continuously trying to escape. And then there were her breasts. They hung full and heavy, and swayed inside the clinging material. There was no way of disguising their perfect rounded shape and large nipples, even if she had wanted to.

"Oh, Jerez, it's beautiful." She ran to him and threw her arms round his neck.

"It's you who are beautiful. The most beautiful woman alive."

"Woman?"

"Most definitely a woman. Only a real woman could wear that dress and make it look like that."

She turned to look at herself again. It was true. With a little more make-up she would look her age. Well, perhaps not, but eighteen anyway. And that was old enough for now. That was officially grown-up.

"Only one thing missing."

She looked at him over her shoulder. Somewhere he had found Oscar and was holding him out to her. She turned to him giggling. "No. I don't think so, Jerez. Sorry, Oscar." She took the bear and gave him a hug and a kiss before handing him back. "But don't go too far away, it can get very dark and scary at night."

Jerez laughed. "Come on, time to go down."

Georgio was sitting in his favourite armchair. He had drawn it closer to the fire and was staring into the flames. As usual the curtains were drawn and the wall lights on. He smiled when she approached, and stood up.

"My goodness!"

She giggled with pleasure.

"Aren't we all grown-up? Let's have a twirl."

She did as she was bid, and walked about the room so that he would have the opportunity to fully appreciate it.

"Stop it, stop it, or I'll never have the heart to let you go."

"Go, Master?" She looked from Georgio to Jerez hoping that this was another trick.

"Yes. You're far too high spirited for us two old codgers, hey, Jerez?"

"Speak for yourself, Sir."

Georgio laughed. "The silly old fool doesn't know his own limitations. He'd be dead in a week, and I don't want to lose him just yet."

"But why, Master. I would be good. I wouldn't let him over exert himself."

"Yes, I saw you doing that this morning. In fact, most of the day, aye, Jerez?" Both men laughed at this.

"But I didn't know then!"

"That's enough. The decision has been made, now behave yourself."

"I'm sorry, Master. But may I ask, where am I to go now?"

"Where would you like to go, my dear?"

"Like to go?"

He nodded, smiling. "If you could choose."

CHAPTER 20

She pressed the bell on the entrance phone. There was a couple of minutes delay while she waited apprehensively, then "Yes, who's there please?" asked a disembodied female voice.

"It's Su - Su - san - Susan Dixon." Christ what a stupid name for someone with a lisp, and an occasional stutter.

The gate clicked open a few inches.

She pushed it, walked inside, and closed it behind her. She walked uncertainly towards the kitchen and the back door. Who's was the unknown voice? Then the back door was thrown open and blonde Margaret was standing there in the sudden blaze of light, beaming at her. Susan raced up the steps and threw herself into her arms.

"So you've come back to us?"

"If he'll have me."

"I don't think you'll have many worries there. He pretends to be a cold fish, but most of it's show. He's a sucker for a pretty face and a sexy body." Margaret laughed. "It's that old witch of a wife you've got to worry about."

"He's married?" Susan was shocked. Why had she never thought of it? Of course he would be married. All the best men are.

"Didn't you know?"

"What's she like?"

"Terrible. Much worse than him. You've got one thing on your side though."

"What's that?"

"She likes little girls."

"Oh. Is that a problem?"

"No. I mean I don't know. I've never tried."

"Don't look so worried, most women haven't."

"Have you?"

"Oh, yes. I love it."

"I wouldn't mind if it was with you."

"Are you sure?"

Susan nodded. She wasn't, but this didn't seem like the right time to have doubts.

"Give us a kiss then."

They kissed. Now she was almost sure. Her head started to buzz and her body reacted immediately. She felt Margaret's hand on her breast and then her leg.

"This is a lot of dress you've got on, lets have it off."

"What here? What if someone was to come in?"

"Who?"

"I don't know."

"Come on, take it off."

Margaret looked at her for a good half minute once the dress was removed.

"God, you're beautiful. Has anyone ever told you that?"

Susan nodded.

"I bet."

Margaret leant forward and kissed each nipple. It was like being struck by lightning. No one had ever been that gentle before.

"Here, come here."

Margaret sat in the rocking chair, then hitched her skirt up and hung her left leg over the arm. Susan looked at her vulva with its covering of soft blond hair. She felt giddy and weak at the knees. Almost without knowing what she was doing she knelt down and put her face between the sweetly perfumed legs. With the first lick of her tongue she knew that she had discovered a new sensation which she would never tire of. She found Margaret's clit and used the very tip of her tongue to coax it out of its shell. Then she took it into her mouth and began to suck. Margaret began to groan and placed both hands on the back of her head pushing it harder against her groin. And Susan began to chew.

It was finished before she wanted it to be.

"Stop, stop, that's enough. You've passed. I can tell you, you do like it."

"As well as, not instead! Oh yes! But - but will I like it with her?"

"Who?"

"His wife."

"Did you like it with me?"

"You know I did!"

"Well then - can't you guess?"

"You mean - you -"

"Of course it's me!"

"Oh, Margaret." Susan fell into her arms. She was so relieved.

"Come on, get your posh frock on, you're going to a party."

"Where?"

"Here. It's your welcome home party."

As soon as they entered the room everyone stopped talking and began to applaud her. She felt herself starting to blush and wanted to turn and run away. But Uncle Peter strode over and took her in his arms. Then Orchid leant forward and pecked her on the cheek. Everyone was crowding round and talking at once, until her master arrived and rescued her.

"How are you?"

"Wonderful, but very scared, Master."

"Of what? Being part of this?"

She nodded. "Yes, Master."

"You needn't be, my dear. You look as elegant and sophisticated as any woman here - and much more beautiful."

"Thank you, Master." She shot a quick glance at the other guests. Was it true? Could she possibly feel at home in this sort of gathering some day?

"Come on, let's go and talk." And he ushered her away into his study.

"We'd better make this formal. Stand in front of the desk."

She did so.

"Well, Susan, when you came to me, you were very naive."

"Yes, Master."

"You had made up your mind to give up your freedom and become my slave."

"Yes, Master."

"I couldn't turn you away. You were too unhappy. God knew what you might do."

She nodded recognising the truth of his words.

"But you knew nothing. You were a little girl in a woman's body."

She nodded again.

"I don't know how much you know now. But you're not a little girl any more. You've blossomed in to the most beautiful woman I've ever seen."

Susan went bright crimson. "Thank you, Master."

"Do you understand why I sent you away Susan?"

"No, Master, I'm sorry, but I don't."

"I had to give you your freedom back. Give you a last chance to decide. Well, that's done now. You've seen a little more of the world."

"Yes, Master. Thank you, Master."

"But have you grown-up enough to be able to make the final decision, as an adult?"

"Yes, Master. I'm sure I have."

"Yes, I think I agree. But then, I think I've always been the only one who had any doubts haven't I?" He grinned at her.

"Yes, Master." Susan's smile was big enough to split her face in two.

"So, what's it to be? Do you want me to tear up your contract and set you free?"

"No, thank you, Master."

He came from behind the desk and she turned towards him so that they were only a couple of feet apart, grinning stupidly at each other.

"Do you want to come here and live as my slave, Susan?"

"Oh yes, yes, yes, Master, thank you, Master. You'll never regret it. I'll be the best slave in all the world, you'll see, and I'll make you the happiest man alive, I swear I will."

He held out his arms, laughing. "Well take that as a yes, shall we?"

"Yes, Master. Thank you, Master, thank you!" She hung on to his neck and he swung her round. And then they kissed.

"There's one thing we haven't done yet!"

The waves of longing and desire returned to her as he unbuckled his belt...

She was complete now, fulfilled.

She soon settled back into the routine. It was strange at first knowing that Margaret was his wife. But she was so kind and considerate and didn't seem to mind at all about Susan loving her husband. In fact, she would have found it strange if anyone didn't. There was less housework for her to do now with two of them to do it and her master didn't seem to mind her being in his study while he was working.

He normally tied her to the pillar nearest his desk, with her arms above her head and just enough tension to make her stand on her toes, so that she was in continuous discomfort. She knew that she mustn't make a sound, unless he asked her opinion about his work.

She lived for the moments when he came and ran his hands over her body, which he often did, especially when things had gone well and he was in a good mood.

Then there came a day when Margaret entered with the second post. As usual, after laying it on his desk and smiling at Susan, she fussed about the room for a while. So they were both there when he opened the hand-written letter. And when he had read it, they both noticed when he placed it in a different tray to usual; one which Susan had never seen him use before.

Margaret crossed to the desk immediately, looking at Susan significantly as she did so. She picked up the letter, but spoke to him before reading it.

"Another one?"

This month's extract is not from our books but from a magazine which includes a new short story by Rex Saviour, author of ERICA, PROPERTY OF REX; Robin, Property of Ogoun, a novelette included in BOUND FOR GOOD; and BALIKPAN 1, ERICA ARRIVES, which is too strong for high street bookshops. This short story shows the author in a softer mood: in the magazine the story is illustrated, (as is a serialisation of Biker's Girl): So here, courtesy of DS Sales, PO BOX CR49 Leeds LS7 3XJ, publishers of (among other things) Balikpan and SM Scene, is:-

SILVER

I was mildly excited when I saw a girl in my headlights, thumbing a lift.

When I saw her rather more clearly through the driving rain, her soaking little skirt clinging to very curvy thighs and her sweater outlining splendidly firm breasts that obviously didn't believe in bras, my excitement rose several notches.

I brought the Jag to a sliding halt beside her, and lowered the electric window.

"Please Mister -"

"Go and stand in the headlights," I said. "Hands above your head! I want to see if you have a gun!"

"Oh but -"

"Now, or I drive on."

She did as I said. What a great little figure! She was barefoot, with a mini skirt, a jersey, lots of long hair, and nothing else. I got out and walked behind her, ran my hands up and down her, not neglecting the breasts that were outlined by the jersey with her hands raised. She shrank away a little but but did not protest.

Definitely no gun. Not even a handbag.

I got back into my seat and beckoned her back to the window.

"What the Hell are you doing out here in the middle of the night?" I asked sternly. "You don't look a day over fourteen!"

"I'm sixteen," she said indignantly, shaking raindrops from her long red hair. "Today, actually!"

"Even so," I said, "I do not approve of young girls out alone at night miles from anywhere." I began to close the window, which, as I expected, put her into a panic.

"You aren't going to leave me? Oh no, Mister, please!"

"I only deal with nice girls," I said. "Obedient ones! What you need is a good spanking, not a lift."

"Oh but Mister -"

"Yes?"

"I am obedient. I like to be obedient, truly I do." The glance she gave me was full of meaning. "I promise to be good, ever so good, I'll do everything you tell me to. Don't leave me out here, all alone, I'm so frightened of the dark. And he took my money -"

"Who?"

"My boy friend I thought he was nice. Then he met another girl at the dance tonight and they just threw me out of the car. I didn't even have my shoes on! And she took my handbag, it had all my money in it." She burst into tears. "And he took my rings and bracelets. People call me Silver, because of all my bracelets, they were my money box."

I opened the door.

"You'd better get in, Silver. I'm getting cold with the window down."

"Not so cold as me, Mister," she snuffled. Now that she was close to me I found her very sexy, sort of slimly plump if you follow me. Juicy. Ripe.

"Don't be cheeky!" I said, "not while you're with me. Doesn't your father ever punish you for being cheeky?"

She shivered. "He used to beat me with his belt when I was naughty, but that's alright because I deserved it."

"Surely you don't think being sixteen changes that?"

"I guess not." She burst into tears again. "My Mum died, you see, and my Dad ran off, so there's nobody to look after me now."

"Or to beat you."

"Well, about that ..." She paused and considered the matter gravely. "A beating or two isn't such a big deal, it would be worth it, wouldn't it, to be looked after real well?"

"Would it?"

She looked at me. I couldn't see what colour her eyes were, but they were big. "Yes, Mister," she said wistfully, "oh yes, it sure would, I don't mind, truly. As a matter of fact ... well, anyway, you plan to beat me, then, if I'm naughty, like I often am? On the bare bum I suppose? Hard, with a strap, like my Dad did?"

When I didn't answer - being speechless, as I'm sure you will appreciate - she leaned over and kissed me, pressing against me, a really erotic experience for a crusty old bachelor like me.

"I miss my Dad," she whispered.

"Where do you live?" I asked when I had got my breath back and my erection a little more comfortably stacked. I also had the car purring gently forward by now.

"I got out of the orphanage this morning, I was going to live with the boy who dumped me. So nowhere, I suppose."

"You'd better come home with me, then, just for tonight," I said.

"I guess so."

"And then we'll see."

"Right!" She started playing with the stereo, apparently quite at home. "Got any good tapes?"

"Yes, opera."

"Holy shit!" She leaned forward and turned on the radio, twiddling until she found reggae, which I detest, and turning it up full blast.

I pulled in to the grassy edge and turned the music off, and she looked at me, her eyes frightened now, no longer mocking, tears not too far away.

"I do not tolerate behaviour like that!" I said. "Over my lap for a spanking, or out! It's up to you!"

"I - I didn't think we were quite that serious," she said.

"Well, I am. Out. Start walking."

"There isn't even room for you to spank me."

"There will be when I come over there and open the door."

"I see." She seemed to be thinking it over. "A spanking or abandoned in the dark, eh? I just hate the dark! So it's a spanking for you, Silver, girl! It's grit your teeth and bear it time! Well, then, Mister, are you still going to take me to your house after you've spanked me?"

"Perhaps. This is a test to see if you are serious about being obedient."

"OK then."

I moved over into her seat, away from the steering wheel, and she came over my lap, surprisingly heavy, just fitting when I opened the door, so that her head was out in the rain and her feet in the driver's seat.

"You really ought to tie me down if you're going to spank me," she said, "because I can't always control myself."

"Maybe another time," I said. I was all a quiver, no breath to talk with, a strange sensation. She was heavy on my penis, wriggling against it a little, and I shifted to get comfortable.

Don't rush this, I said to myself. Fate has dealt you a good 'un. Make the most of it. Test her out properly and maybe ... maybe she will come to live with you and you can spank her once a week.

One hand confirmed that she had no bra and the other was poised to lift that pathetic little rag of a skirt, and yet I couldn't quite do it.

"Knickers," I said.

She twisted her head round.

"You'd better take your knickers off."

"I don't have any, Dumbo."

"And don't be cheeky - I've told you before." I think she was testing me out, seeing how far she could go. Well, she'd soon find out!

"What's your name, then, Dumbo?" she asked.

"Stephen."

"OK Sir Stephen, let's get on with it."

"What's all this about Sir Stephen?"

"He's in my favourite book, the Story of O. Don't you know it, Sir?"

I didn't.

"Well, then," she said, "I think this is going to be fun. I shall call you Sir Stephen and think of myself as 'O'. Carry on, Sir Stephen, do your worst!"

She was trying hard to sound as if she didn't care what I did to her, but there was a very satisfactory tremble in her seductive little voice, and she was squirming against my swollen prick all the time.

Lovely!

But I couldn't hold out much longer, and then the thrill would be gone.

"Pull your skirt up."

"Well -"

"NOW!"

"Yes, Sir, I am your obedient servant. I do like your beard, it makes you ever so fierce."

Two timid little hands came and pulled the skirt slowly back, revealing the plumpest little bottom I have ever seen, an arse to shame all arses!

"Hold your skirt there."

"How many are you going to give me?"

"We'll see, won't we? As many as I think necessary, OK?"

"OK," she said, but her voice was definitely trembling now.

I put a finger on her flesh and felt her jump. I traced a circle with my thumb nail. I would have to speed up, or I would erupt and spoil it all.

But when I got her home ...

"If this all the clothes you have?" I asked. "This bit of a skirt and the jersey? No knickers, no bra?"

"That's all I was wearing, that's what my pig of a boy friend liked. Will you buy me some clothes, Sir?"

"Perhaps. Shoes, anyway. When we get home you can take these wet things off. They're filthy anyway. I think I'll burn them."

"What will I wear?"

"I'll think I can spare you a shirt."

"Oh, but -"

"You aren't nearly as tall as I am, so it will be quite decent for a while. And the house is very warm."

"Yes, but -"

"I will not be argued with!" I confess to licking my lips. "So I've changed my mind. Take the skirt and jersey off now!"

"Oh but -"

"NOW! Or get out and walk!"

She looked out into the dark wet night and then I slid back into my seat whilst she struggled out of her wet things without another word.

"Throw them out, then close the door."

To my amazement, she did as she was told without further protest, and then actually put her arms round me and gave me a kiss!

I had left the engine running to keep us warm, and now I drove on in silence. When I glanced at her in the dim starlight I got an impression of firm high breasts, not too big, definitely not too small.

"Now you'll have to look after me!" she said contentedly.

"Is that what that kiss was for?"

"Yes, you're my guardian now, my benefactor. Perhaps I'll be your slave-girl, because you definitely can't abandon me like this! And at least your slave girl doesn't get to be spanked!. That's a relief! I rather think you meant to hurt!"

"I did," I said. I drew in to the verge again. "I do."

"Holy shit!"

"Quite. Stop talking all this rubbish and come over my lap as before."

It was even more delicious this time, specially the hand that held a breast, quite different without a jersey between. Her nipple was real hard, the little minx!

I ran my other hand up and down inside those splendid legs of hers, making her open them. She wouldn't be very tall, I suppose, I could tell better in daylight, but she was certainly beautifully rounded, warm and already squirming delightfully under my roving fingers, giving a little squeal or two and a special wriggle when my fingers reached her delicate bits, but not protesting.

She was actually soaking wet, as if she was enjoying what I was doing! I pushed a finger in, and all she did was wriggle.

A very amenable girl - or maybe she really did have a phobia about the dark.

I raised my hand and brought it down hard, with a satisfactory slap.

"Ow," she said, "that hurt!" A hand came feeling for the place to rub it better.

"Keep your hands out of the way," I said. "Or the stroke won't count."

"But I don't know how many I'm going to get!"

"Never mind, I still advise you to keep your hands away."

I didn't know how many she would be getting either. I intended to keep going until my orgasm, but it couldn't be much delayed. No doubt I'd do better with practise, improve my control and all that.

After three hard slaps she began to cry softly, then to sob openly. Very stimulating. I was on the verge of flooding.

After six she was heaving about like mad and howling without restraint. She had good lungs, but there wouldn't be anyone within miles of us.

"Holy shit!" she screamed. "I didn't bargain for this! I thought you were a soft touch!"

She tried to wriggle away from me, but I had her in a grip that was much too hard for her. I am pretty strong, actually, and tall - over six feet. Only my orgasm could save her now I had my dander up.

Slap! Slap! Slap! I began to lay into her really hard and fast, and she was really screaming and squirming, squirming and screaming, struggling like mad, all her bottom quivering and juddering, oh it was so lovely ... She tried to bite me, but I easily stopped that and increased my pace and vigour, slap, slap, slap, slap.

Then I exploded, best ever, on and on and on, heaving up and down beneath her naked belly!

As my breathing eased and my heart slowed, she wriggled round and came and nestled into my arms, snuggling up and still crying softly.

At last she spoke.

"Well, then, you are really going to look after me, aren't you? I was ever so good, wasn't I?"

"If I can train you to my ways, make you into a real good obedient companion."

"Well, yes, OK Sir, whatever turns you on, I'm your helpless victim, aren't I, I'll have to be your loving kitten or your little dog or your pony or your absolutely obedient slave-girl, but not to beat me that hard next time, my God that really hurt!"

"We'll see!" I said.

She would squirm great under the slipper, I thought.

And as for the belt ...

I would be good with the belt, I thought.

She would have to ask me very nicely if I was to go easy on that!

We'd soon find out how submissive she could be!

DS Sales sell Balikpan 1 at £10 including postage, and SM Scene by subscription

All Silver Moon and Silver Mink titles available from shops £4.99 or (USA $ - varies) or direct (UK) £5.60 including postage or (USA) $6.95 + $2.95 per parcel

ISBN 1-897809-01-8 BARBARY SLAVEMASTER
ISBN 1-897809-02-6 ERICA:PROPERTY OF REX
ISBN 1-897809-99-9 BALIKPAN 1:ERICA ARRIVES*
ISBN 1-897809-03-4 BARBARY SLAVEGIRL
ISBN 1-897809-04-2 BIKER'S GIRL
ISBN 1-897809-05-0 BOUND FOR GOOD
ISBN 1-897809-07-7 THE TRAINING OF SAMANTHA
ISBN 1-897809-08-5 BARBARY PASHA
ISBN 1-897809-09-3 WHEN THE MASTER SPEAKS**
ISBN 1-897809-10-7 CIRCUS OF SLAVES
ISBN 1-897809-11-5 THE HUNTED ARISTOCRAT
ISBN 1-897809-13-1 AMELIA**
ISBN 1-897809-14-x BARBARY ENSLAVEMENT
ISBN 1-897809-15-8 THE DARKER SIDE**
ISBN 1-897809-16-6 RORIG'S DAWN
ISBN 1-897809-17-4 BIKER'S GIRL ON THE RUN
ISBN 1-897809-19-0 TRAINING OF ANNIE CORRAN**
ISBN 1-897809-20-4 SONIA**
ISBN 1-897809-21-2 THE CAPTIVE**
        *Direct only, £10 ($15)   **Silver Mink

Silver Moon Reader Services
PO Box CR25, Leeds LS7 3TN
or
PO Box 1614, New York NY 10156

FREE BOOKLET OF EXTRACTS ON REQUEST